Arreshy Young

CODON

Arreshy Young

ISBN 978-1-940853-37-6

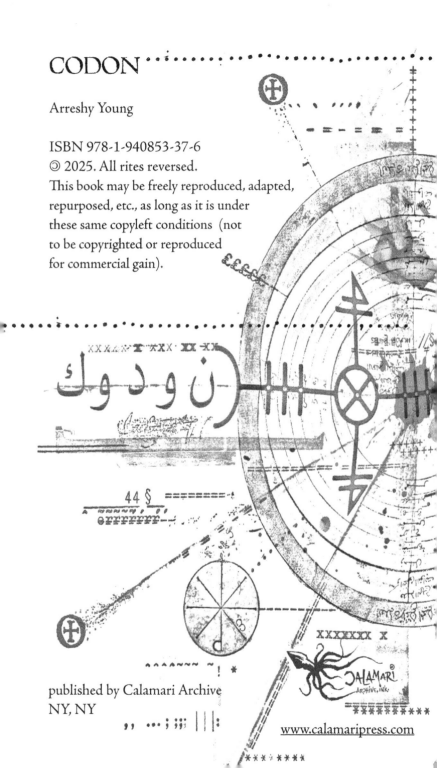

published by Calamari Archive
NY, NY

www.calamaripress.com

CONTENTS:

FVNVERAL STORIES

Monomeron

Postscript to a speech delivered at the *23rd International Majlis and Retrospective on Medicine,* Hotel Kerkur, Colonial Cherfis, 298 D.E.:

"I recall that Sa'di said, 'A person wept the livelong night beside a sick man's bed: when it dawned the Sick was well, and the mourner, he was dead.' And then it occurred to me, too late to add to my lecture, that there is one way in which the aqala-doctor has merited the respect due to the Great Reconciliators— Buddha, Solon, Salman, Hallaj. We have made loyalty possible in times of plague. Historically, compassion for the Contagious was impossible. To betray one's friends was not a choice. Either a man abandoned them willingly or by catching the disease and dying."

~~The Death of PSC Cenote Lancôme~~

Has been revoked.

The so-called "death" we attribute to the mass delusion of crowds (LSD in the CHQ water reservoir? Organizations wishing to claim responsibility for the attack are invited to apply at the link below).

For as is stated by Ajami Private Diction law "the legal <u>person</u> status of the **Private Service Commune** gives them perpetual life, the deaths of syndics or cellholders do not alter the commune's biological function." No matter how many psychedelic cellholders claim they have "died" by ballistic affliction imposed by subversive hallucinations, rest assured we are forever. Your service packs will be delivered on time and with the same indulgent altruism as before.

⊕

Noise Control

> "And that was the death of Hip Hop."
> —The Hezerdja Register of Historical Astrology

⊕

Do you wish to give admin permissions to the IHSAN Project Management Tool?

```
Main Menu > Add New Social User Story
```

Description: As a Virtue Administrator, I would like to reduce city noise pollution to soothe resident complaints, which have risen to the level of a social problem.

Dev Notes: <u>Noise</u>—etymologically in English "the sound of a musical instrument." Old French—sense of <u>riot</u>, of the kind which have lately afflicted the Virtuous City coinciding with "le grande derange," the uninhibited infestation by no-minder ~~scum~~ weeds with their frenzy inducing harmonies.

Preconditions: Sufficient distributive nozzle density in infested areas

Execution Plan: Organic Rebranding Algorithm

Deployment Method: Social Bacteriophage (Cutter Genome)

Viral Load: 3,000,000 copies / ml

Authorization Notes: Executed under Social Synod decret-loi #SS4359-A. Targeted rebranding approved.

Action Report: Synthesis_Episcript_SS4359A_17_B.eps

Sample Code:

```
1.  var credentials = CertificateContext.
    GetCredentials()),
2.  var AJPD = ActiveIntellectAPI.
    AjamiPrivateDictionFactory.GetInstance(epochId),
3.
4.  /**** Linguistic rebranding ****/
5.
6.  //music = noise, etymologically.
7.  AJPD.EthicalContext.
    Rebrand(hipHopDefinitionID, (EthicalContext.
    GetDefinition_Encrypted(noiseDefinitionID,
    credentials));
8.
9.  //Broader rebranding approval pending.
10. /* AJPD.EthicalContext.
    Rebrand(musicDefinitionID, */
11.
12. //eliminate redundancy
13. AJDP.EthicalContext.Delete(noiseDefinitionID);
14.
15.
16. /**** Physiological rebranding ****/
17. var weedsTargetList = WeedsAPI.GetList_
    Encrypted(userStoryID, credentials);
18.
19. var soundAssociationList = new List()
    { SoundLibrary.PoliceSiren,
20. SoundLibrary.CougarSnarl, SoundLibrary.
    DiveBomberScream };
21.
```

```
22. AJPD.PhysiologicalContext.AuralContext.
    PanicResponse.Link(hipHopDefinitionID,
23. soundAssociationList, weedsTargetList);
24.
25. /**** Synthesis ****/
26. SocialPharmacologyContext.Synthesize(AJPD.
    EthicalContext.RebrandingDictionary_Changes,
    credentials);
```

Acceptance Criteria: Noise Reduction > 98%.

Systems Log:
DDoS attack deflected.
Volume overload attack detected. Septic cross-shunting initiated.
Recombinant synthesis (monomer partition) initiated...
Cell sniffing detected. Broad pheromone defense initiated.
Bacteriophage gestation counter: 177568.
Scheduled cardiac drive defrib, executing...
Waterhole attack detected. Infected employee voluntary apology tour and termination phases 1 through 7 approved.
Bacteriophage gestation counter: 688568.

Crudo

The easiest way to crack your crudo style frozen egg is don't. Don't do it! Instead, rhythmically tap (gently now!) the egg with a plastic spoon to wake the sleeping chick. Once you hear the "peep," place egg in well-oiled bowl. Be patient and let the hatching instinct take over.

While you wait, mix lime juice, garlic salt, cumin and a dab of Hassiba cuck-pepper sauce in a shot glass and set aside. The chick's adorable escape attempts should coat it nicely.

Drizzle chickadee bald patch with aioli then stuff in mouth and hold. For an extra electric tang, allow chick to peck around your tongue for a bit. Then right as it begins to melt, swallow whole. Shoot the chaser.

If properly gestated, the initial meta-gravy dribblings will congeal into the most pristine gobs and giblets you've ever tasted.

For a candied twist (a dessert version of "yemas de Santa Hallaj"), shorten gestation period in the alembic dyncubator™ from four weeks to one. Instead of oil, coat bowl with confectioners' sugar. Right as chick starts to melt, roll with chunks of ginger and candied cherries until evenly coated. The moisture will help it stick. For advanced home cooks, an intravenous cream filling can be a delightful alternative.

⊕

Foodie Nation

Let us not forget Chef Gallois, a man who gave birth to an entire generation of test tube chefs from his inseminated taste buds.

⊕

Orientalit

A group of Orientalists inhale a burning copy of *One Thousand and One Nights*.

⊕

The Trumpet Cutter

Dad opened the GIF. "Is that what the virus looks like? It looks like a ball of carpet hair with trumpets sticking out. Is that how the vaccine works? Does it cut off the trumpets?"

Is this a dad joke? An Old Testament patriarch joke?

The Holy Spirit is a contract ventriloquist. It's her job to speak through everybody, but she works odd hours. Like when, immediately after said dad joke, I "accidentally" ("accident" in the

Aristotelian sense of unnecessary, circumstantial, not adhering by definition to the human species) hit the CAPS LOCK key while googling, then accidentally ("accident" now in the Proustian sense of a probability shitstorm of collateral damage which I will only reconstruct, wrongly, in memory) double-tapped the touchpad with my unsprained right wrist (the cast on my left hand reeks like slaughterhouse cheddagogue about to be devoured alongside an iconic Hannibal the Cannibal wine pairing) before I can finish typing "the ending to Karate Kid 2 live or die man nose honk." So that I end up with 1117 search results about the "THE END," i.e. the End Times, the Last Judgment, the necrotic struggle for survival which evolves Bipedal Death with Thumbs.

Search result #88 turns out to be the first one that's not about the pandemic or an ingratiating "Dear Ignatius" advice column for inquiring street preachers but an essay about one of the least bee-buzzyng of William Blake's 537 watercolors executed for Edward Young's *Night Thoughts*. In it, a pool diving angel (silver medalist teetering on bronze) trumpets "Last Call" or "You made out with who???" to a wasted or detoxing skeleton snoozing or boozing under a funeral shroud. Presumably the skeleton will be tartared in a formal meat suit (filleted from the damned, one skin fits all) before interviewing with his Maker. Heaven has a strict flesh code.

So maybe Dad's funny after all.

I remind you that people like my dad, venerated Nobel Prize fanboy and small-cap microbiologist, are your last best hope during this plague of last judgment trumpet viruses.

Bibliophilia or The Bordello of Dead Books

Grave robbing. "The Female Revolutionary Plutarch" with curved spine and ample spine hubs.

She huffs a wolfish puff to clear the dust. She rubs the red rot powder across her ears and breasts, glides the silk bookmark down from neck to gut, gut to _____, caresses the calfskin binding, sniffs the paper, talks dirty in dead languages. She spreads the textblock with her tongue. Spits coyly on the frontispiece. Wets her fingers to better turn the pages. Sniffs the fingers that turn the pages. Slides her fingers a second and third time back into her _____.

She binds and blinds herself with book binder's tape and scissors the textblock, whispering blasphemies and coquetries, doing her best to redirect any discharge into the pubic dispensers pegged around the reading room. She edges close five times. Then, right as she is about to give up, hits the pitch, twitching like a tuning fork, hearing loss, squealing in binary orangutan, le petit morts.

"Times up," Madame Librarian calls.

She slides a lit cigarette into the book as a bookmark. Madam Librarian clucks and pinches out the flame.

On her way out, she passes a man in a gimp suit (underneath he was, perhaps, a dehydrated thirst trap). They both titter politely, pretending to be nervous to put each other at ease.

<u>We're all sex positive. No need to freak out.</u>

⊕

The Death of a Funeral

(Funeral redacted).

⊕

Leather Bound

In his wasiya will he specified that his posthumous biography be bound in leather tanned from himself.

⊕

Ad-Bot

Flash Sale. Preorder, 15% off. Your favorite sword and sandal Pokémon return! Pokémon Pontius Pilate EX Sapphire Collection. "Gotta crucify them all!" Blood Libel (Protocols of Zion) and NWO Agenda DLCs available for separate download.

Dank Memes

Tab one. Album Drop. The twitch trance band "Sugaring Blowout" drops 500 vinyl copies of their unsellable album "Fidgeital Romance" onto doomed pedestrians from the 40th floor of the Hotel Hibel.

Tab two. Resting Goth Face.

```
1. <animation images="face_smile_noMakeup.jpg,
   face_GothMakeup.jpg" transitionMode=
   "lenticularHologram" transitionDelaySeconds =
   "2" />
```

Tab three. A dank meme referring to that one house party where the serial monogamist with the pussy-parcher spouse tears out her own tongue and gives herself a little twing-twang in the bathroom. While emptying out the trash can, the host finds Missy Monogamist's lips, sans lip ring, still puckering a wet blunt.

Death of a Deepfake Dreamer

The Dreamer trips into an ephemeral meat grinder. His posthumous dream keeps on dreaming, harvesting his recombinant gore to reproduce 16 deepfake test tube babies.

Darwinia

A spider monkey crashes to the ground and dies. From the toxic soil, the angelim trees no longer grow in unbroken rows, but the spider monkeys jump with undiminished hope.

Funeral Wear

The insect wears its skeletal coffin. All insects are crawling funerals. Their funerals are funerals attending funerals.

Mass Christ Party

The Mass Christ party was winding down.

Every Jesus had brought his Judas. Every Judas had brought his nails. Their electric drills, by Dubayr™, were anachronistic but fuck, it was a party right?

All the Jesuses—Goth-Cross, Baroque, Post-Menopausal Jesus, Double Agent Social Justice Jesus, Satanist Jesus, Incel Jesus, Creampunk Christ, Sufi Alcoholic Jesus, HR Hivemind Jesus, Mermicorn Jesus, Clustercluck Chicken AI Jesus, Slut-shaming Jesus, Slutty Jesus, a Cinnamon Toast Christ, Ethical Polyam Jesus, Holographic Jesus, Marshmallow Jesus ("This is my body. Roast it with chocolate and graham crackers in remembrance of me.")—sent their lamentations up to their Everlasting Dad as each Judas drilled them hard to their pastel-chalk-art concrete crosses, each Jesus swiftly bleeding out.

Mitochondriarchy or The Mitochondriac's Safety Guide

...statistically, our ruined economy is no more than Berkeley's "ghost of departed quantities." But I do not have to understand my country. I have only to love her and confess that to me she is still a "machine beloved for its fatal qualities."

Enough of this.

My analysis of the Sanhadjan penal code you will find, after a brief prolegomena on The Republic, on pages 187–227 of my report, which I hope will assist the Commission in the passage of enlightened prison reform so sorely necessary to soothe the present abuses and disorders. In response to your last letter, I can only respond that I dare not—and I hope you will come to agree with me or even admire me in this, my holographic suicide—exert on the Commissioners, elected ra'wis of the people, any influence on the basis of mere hereditary "skyminder prerogative, noblesse oblige must burn on the same pyre with the nobles.

As to my personal Muqaddimah, the "meat" as you call it, on the forlorn bones of political science, I can here only encode a few dominant strands of DNA, an episcript in want of a polymerist. A coded query packet for delivery to Assidi Ilyas, Hatoshi Publishing PSC, will follow, when I feel the time is ripe.

And the World is growing ripe.

Even now the hyenas of Reaction gather to rip the revolutionary organism from its womb, to raise from its recombinant gore a World-Conqueror to save their skins. And yet millions have already heard the birth pangs, a squalling from another world. What form will this new organism assume?

Will it be the data-driven Binarchy of Outremer, with its elected algorithms?

Or the Military Ochlocracy of Akhua, with its 3-headed Mob—the godskin petcheneg, the Social Synod with its "social" veto (i.e. "bulldozing powers"), the religious pasquinade, the ulema-adjutors of the Radiant Imaad?

The Sod? The gendered tyranny of a benevolent world-organism who compels each Deu Ames and their sacrificial saints towards <u>asabiyya</u>—slavery to the living soil. For have you not heard? "A herd that huddles together trembling in the presence of danger, a child that clings weeping to its mother, a man desperately striving to force a way into his god—all these are seeking to return out of the life of freedom into the vegetal servitude from which they were emancipated into individuality and loneliness."

Or will it be Sanhadja Siyaasah? Sanhadja, whose suborbital sophisms about "cell division" (mitosis of the polity) sound moon-mad to the dirt-minder school of "realism" but which nevertheless conceal a fever for liberty so epidemical in its spread and so blessed in its symptoms that I say to you now: let me be diseased!

As to you, I hear reports that in the grand tradition you are an office seeker denying that she is seeking office. A friend's advice, drop the pretense. Your virtues are known to many, to me above all, and the Consulate needs candor and leadership more than patriotic humility.

With Affectionate Regard,

Bint Haruko Tomayashi, Saksiwa Consulate, Satellite Bureau

Postscript.

And here, as promised, germline chapter headings equivalent to "working" titles:

Law or The Bones of Their FathersLiberty and The Blessed Geology of Sanhadja

Revolution or The Permanent Conspiracy

Concord (Ijma'a) and Synthesis

Cell Division or The Ontology of Secession

The Phases of Mitosis

The Eight Year Law or Cell Recombination

The People's Power, Upper and Lower Congeries

The People's Physiology

Ihya or The Biology of the Religious Sciences
The Greatness of the Prize or Congenital Defects
The World Conqueror or The Threat of Akhua

⊕

...Akio snickered. He climbed up the rickety ladder and tossed
the book into the mouth of the moloch incinerator to imaginary
applause.

Fraternity. Equality. And fucking book critiques. Ha. Ha.

Shit, the fumes were making him dizzy. Better get down. He'd
done his job, above the call, checking checklists double-time, but
he'd hardly been able read past his yawns. The patriotic toyminder
crowds had all shot their loads and mogged off to comb the sewers
for skyminder rats to kill, an old-school ratonnade.

Fuck me, I should have gone with them. Not that they would
let a bugminder crawl along. Fraternity..."frat" chance.

He laughed at his own pun, but really he was just bored,
so goddamn bored and decaffeinated and the PSC firewall
was airtight despite the hax his friend had guaranteed "on his
revolutionary balls" would work. He needed to blow off steam.

"I earned it," he muttered. He was sure he had seen the
nightshift guard hide a porno-mag in some chub-duct somewhere.
And the maphrians swore they had scraped their spy-eyes from
the bathroom stalls. If not...whelp, hope they're ready for a show.

⊕

The School of Athens

Among Alexander the Great's tutors, the Tutor [Aristotle] of his
tutors excluded, we find...[there is a lacunae in the text, lagoons of
lacunae to be honest]:

"...there is Dicaearchus, the unlucky plagiarist of
Theophrastus. Either Caesar or the caliph Omar or a natural
firestorm is said to have burned his surviving manuscripts

together with the entire library of Alexandria in order to escape a siege or to extirpate idolatry or to justify the laws of meteorology."

From Varro we learn that Dicaearchus believed that mind and memory do not exist, that <u>mind</u> is a succession of transitory biochemical configurations. Our imagined memories, including those of remembering, are "a basilisk of earth and water" produced by the universe changing and deranging our bodies. Strictly speaking, our memories are real but never reproduce themselves.

Or as the philosopher himself puts it, obliquely, "At one moment, I am Dicaearchus remembering a kiss. The next moment I am a different Dicaearchus with a baseless suspicion that once I had been kissed."

⊕

Baizizan Wushiwuzizan or a 55-Word Elegy for the Aral Sea

"The Aral, fed in antique days by the fourth river of Paradise. In Alexander's time, landlocked, inexhaustible, its 1,100 islands spotted with pirate havens, unassailable but by a fleet carried overland from Orenburg and reassembled on shore. Thanks to Soviet irrigation projects, the eastern basin has dried, it is now the inexhaustible Aralkum Desert."

⊕

The Vnified Theory of Cuddling/Cuckolding

According to the hostile translation of Bar Huthayl, a beta-testing god is an incel.[1] Unfuckable from its perspective, and who dares doubt the word of god?

Yet god in his mercy has provided three proofs to soothe our doubts as follows:

The "Proof Theological" is elucidated by the orthodox theologians who assert, not without acrimony, that: "God cannot

---

[1] A victim of ishq-desire, "the bitterness of desire in the unsatisfied she-camel," according to Louis Massignon.

be loved, because He cannot love Himself. For to be loved would humanize God. It is blasphemous to anthropomorphize God."

The "Proof Electrostatic" by induction reduces to the following equation:

$$F = \frac{(Q_1 + Q_2)}{(4\pi\varepsilon_0 \, r^2)}$$

Which Bint Zaliza, the celebrated infinitesimal poetess interprets as: "We touch but do not touch, fuck but do not fuck. So the pandars of electrostatic forces attest. The more our particles attract, the more they repel until our loathing could repel the God of Love Himself."

The "Proof Etymological" by deduction presents greater difficulties in that the premises are reputed weak but still attested by the bare minimum of three nahwi of undoubted veracity: God is a unity. In no way is He fractional. Or if fractional, he hates all women undividedly. A Unity is a Whole Number. More rigorously, God is an Integer, One wholly Good and Positive. Etymologically "Integer" means Untouchable.

And its corollary: If untouchable, god cannot touch himself. QED.

Thus the pent-up rage. Thus God kills the little Egyptian sons to spite the women who rejected Him or to eliminate future rivals. Thus Lot is moved by the virile Holy Spirit to give up his daughters to the Sodomites rather than his male guests (angels incognito). Thus the affliction of Mary. Thus either Joseph or Gabriel knocks Mary up, despite her taking "every precaution." And thus her fetus is deemed unabortable by popular demand despite her recourse to tools and methods that Tertullian would have condemned and Augustine would have allowed, with reservations and prudent ambiguities, in the first trimester. Thus all angels are male-leaning, even the Pre-Raphaelite cherub and nephilim are twinks or transitioning. Thus He afflicts the World with St. Paul, trained from infancy to clever legalizing in order to bar women from the ministry, though they are allowed to serve punch at potluck dinners (love feasts, so-called). Thus He sends the rains, His deepfake tears, a flash flood to "baptize" and drown all the snooty hot girls and their <u>asshole</u>, <u>douchebag</u>, <u>cuck</u> boyfriends who are undoubtedly making fun of Him whenever He is busy fantasizing about moving out of the celestial basement of Alpha Testing God, His more athletic Father.[2]

The Wedding Jug

Once, two merchants got into an argument over the respective merits of their indistinguishable import-export dogmas. The second merchant killed the first. The local jurisconsult ruled it "a point of honor" and declined to prosecute. Assessing his merits/demerits God judged the second merchant too unremarkable to replug into a living body and so put his soul into a wine jug of average loveliness.

The years passed. The second merchant, by Fortune's whim, was betrothed to the daughter of the Dawla ambassador to the Tajlideeya dynastic heresiarchs.

With half the dowry, the merchant planned a wedding feast, inviting all the abna al-dunya (the beau monde of that distant era) and their poet-parasites to attend. But the costs soon spiraled out of control and the merchant found that half, or even all, the dowry was not enough to feed the guests and also buy the broidered cushions, tustari carpets, porcelain bowls, peacocks, jugglers, handsome rabbit-boys, curcuna dancing clowns, fire-breathers, cengi-harpists, mimes.

Now both the merchant and the ambassador were in hock to the imperial bank to support their lavish lifestyles, but the merchant saw no recourse but further usury. So he sent an agent to the sayarifa money-changers and began to carve away the lard

---

[2] This last clause may be an interpolation by Gnostic-leaning cults [Cf. the Valentinian dogma of 88 decreasingly defective Gods in Qittmir, pg. 67. —editor]

of extravagance. Fewer gems and anklets for the dancers, brass instead of gold bangles for the rabbit-boys, smaller elephants, hagridden peacocks, day old flowers. He cut and cut, down to the copper cherubim, but it became obvious that at this rate he would have to invite his creditors to gorge and drink their fill every day of their lives just to defer the interest on all his loans.

And the wine! The merchant tore off his beard and with the hairs he wove a prayer mat in the dust. The wine...there he could not penny-pinch. What aristocrat could be fooled by cheap wine when it was an iron law of skyminder manners that by the age of five every ottamati-heir should know his Kerkur dries from his Gurjan wets, his steel-aged sherries from his Garameyni casks?

And the merchant made plans to mortgage his summer villa, 18 haath of olive groves, 12 high-bred horses, 4 of his high-bred concubines.

Just then the merchant's faithful seneschal-wakil, seeing his master's distress, swore on the Most High that he knew a vintner who could supply wine at ¼ -price that even the most eminent tasters of the Dawla court could not distinguish from the grapes of Paradise.

And so the seneschal hurried to Tashabah Suuq. And the tragic consequences of his vow are known to all. But by Fortune's whim the seneschal was able to strike a deal with his supplier friend and bought 200 knockoff jugs, a demi-seraphim of gold for every ten, filled with slightly spoiled wine masked by otherworld spices of such supernal splendor that his competitors accused him of dealings with the infernals.

Feast-day came. The guests arrived.

Among the favored parasites was a beardless wool carder named Hallaj who appeared to be trying to dodge small talk and his mother. He had recently gained access to certain pious abna al-dunya Madames entertained by his religious frenzies and odd conspiratorial doctrines expressed in esoteric orangutan and a cryptic vocabulary. At that moment he was deep in thought, a young man of deep ambition and deep delusions, of deeper hatred for the rich skyminders that fed and petted him for their amusement and set him in their boudoirs as a pious lucky charm, an up and coming revolutionary prophet working out a new publicity campaign funded by his high class dupes and centered around a catchphrase that was sure to stir up the Mob.

"Something about roses and gloves?" he muttered. "No…I bring not doves but hawks?" He was still trying to work out the kinks. Most of all he needed to perform an act of such gross criminality that it would shock the People out of their stupor and announce his apostolic coming of age.

Just then his mother tracked him down, nagging and throwing powdered myrrh across his armpits and neck to mask the smell of wool and dung. Sighing, the wool carder fended her off and started to pour himself a cup of wine, stopped, sniffed the cup, blinked and rubbed the fatty flaps (like the choicest cuts of Abel's flock) beneath his eyes and shook the crust from his anointed lashes and gaped at the crowd as if awakening from a nap during some celestial sermon. For here it was. His predestined enemies in a single Mob, all the abna al-dunya, princes, atabegs, musicians, phlyarchs, dynasts and their mawla clients. All here to get drunk and here was the wine.

He grabbed one of the jugs. By Fortune's malice, that jug had lain unsold for years in the Tashabah Suuq and he still remembered his former life as a wealthy merchant struck down mid-flight. And with a prayer the wool carder performed his only miracle and changed the wine to diarrhea water (in that era all water was diarrhea water) without, however, changing the color.

The newly baptized son of chaos repeated this for all the jugs and then faked a stomach flu and fled.

And here we end the tale, for the uplifting ending is known to all.

⊕

Skin Care Tontine

She lost her faces day by day. These earlobes that Vera
Yemelyanov bit like knockoff silver nephilim, these cheeks she
scissored knuckles down, her lips grazing through these lips
in search of fresh strawberries, finding none and so the futile-
fragrant hunt goes on.

Anya pinched the cheek. Two new wrinkles, crow's feet,
youth-eaters. Each day this face would die and rise a little older,
until it became a Baba Yaga ogress who hid herself in a cowardly
chicken-legged house. The Baba Yaga in that painting by Victor
Vasnetsov for whose epic ugliness Anya's tweenage-soul had felt
a violent solidarity which had never really mellowed, despite her
grudging veneration for beauty's mesmeric powers, seeing then
that her own undine loveliness was only a passing tyranny over
the human hag.

The tweezers chilled her hands with the malice of porcelain
toilet lids. She plucked her right eyebrow. As she plucked the left,
it peeled right off, swirling like an eagle feather, omen of some
emperor's death.

That's not right. Neither were her tidal forehead folds
supposed to crash nor veiny kraken drag ships of screaming baby
fat, nor her cheeks prune that fast, nor gas emit like that from her
melting chin to sting her eyes and balloon her sagging eyelid flaps.

That's not right. Necrosis ran, bipedal Death with thumbs.

And then she realized her grave mistake. She had been
powdering this face with babushka's ashes. Had Vera switched the
labels? She reapplied a binding foundation. By then half her nose
was swirling down the sink.

Fuck. They never should have stored babuskha in a plastic
"urn," especially not one indistinguishable from a dozen other
planet-pleasing recycled bottles filled with the de-aging ashes
of famous beauties handed down by a dreadful wasiya legacy to
babuskha's trembling granddaughters (some snitch had told the
tariqa maphrian about the cremation and crazy chrome-dome

Father-Mother Slovetsky Slimane had interrupted the Eucharist, of all things, to throw homiletic firebolts down on their kopfs for the blatant insult to the Russian Orthodox tenets enjoining burial established by the 88th Conventicle of S_P-burg, Mechta Nouveau, 37 D.E.).

Anya resisted the urge to ping her sisters. They had divided all but babushka's ashes (each cindercule a crystal ankh of power) evenly between themselves. Babushka, they had blithely pushed on her as the elder childe, only suggesting that such lowly "accommodations" as a plastic bottle might mortify their self-born matriarch enough to repress her skyminder malevolence until such time as death anointed the wasiya legacy's final owner.

No, this "grave mistake" was best confessed to the mirror and no one else. Every mea culpa, as Eve foresaw, was a potential curse. Her sisters, though they adored each other, would only interpret this supposed fuck-up as an opening gambit.

She would deal with Vera. Vera who loved the moon for its madness and madness for its moonliness.

<u>Who kneads me, when I am ashes, is my chit in wishes.</u> Her ritual tears ran with the skin cells.

The Flower Maker

According to Bint Marjane Sanjil, who heard it from her father Bar Moloud Sanjil in the year he was excised from his twin brother by the priest-eater Bar Yaqub: "We are told that a fakir of Narada, renowned for holy madness, cut off his nose and left it in the plastic gardens of the Flower Maker, so fearful was he that its aromas were planting not rapture but hellfire in his soul. Others—hostile traditionists—accuse the recluse of wishing to intoxicate himself at all hours with the garden's perfume. So that whether the fakir had to leave in order to beg or to perform gaudy charisms to beguile the Mob or to induce, through ingestion of rare poisons, epileptic ecstasies to strengthen his oracular reputation, or even should the spoiled meat of his body fly up to the inferior gardens of Paradise, his nose might be left behind to inhale with severed sensile nostrils the Flower Maker's supernal orchids, his roses, his dahlias.

Such was the Flower Maker's godlike skill that his warring wives would conspire together to pluck out a polyurethane petal or split a limpid stem before delivering bouquets to his customers, wary that excessive perfection might draw the jealous attention of the infernal sons of Harut and Marit, whose gardening skills, above the moon, were proverbial.

It didn't help that there were so few rivals worth being jealous of. For the Makers of those days were mostly fossil makers, mimers of the dead, mothers of stillborn art.

Because of this, the Flower Maker's customers were all the more eager to blow his reputation from east to west with the fierceness of a Coriolis wind.

One grateful fiscal scribe proclaimed that the scent of the Flower Maker's orchids "grew on him" and, denying that this was mere poetic license, displayed his extra nostrils to his gaping guests. "Surely," he declaimed, "I have obtained new organs of sense beyond those which the wise Galen has anatomized from his sacrilegious dissections and the Second Teacher Faraabi has likened to the virtuous organs of the perfect State."

The trignometrix and astronomer Bint Kantura gave up the study of the heavens for botanics and claimed she had teased the smell of Venus and Mars from the anthers of the Flower Maker's buds and would soon produce a star chart in smells which would predict the orbital revolutions of the planets impelled by their love for god.

And so each customer tried to express in their own private vocabulary what they felt. Some likened it to a demon possession, others to the moment just before a failed orgasm or the ecstasy when one takes a pious wound in holy war, or squeezing from their mothers' wombs, or the drooling caused by that first whiff of baking bread after a famine.

And it came about that the rich let their natural gardens wither and the poor bugminders of the cities dug up their feeble herbs and tubers ("nourishing" by legal definition) and farmers burned their crops so as not to mingle their wretched stink with the Flower Maker's gardenias, the only of the Flower Maker's flowers that a bugminder could afford. And for the same reasons the wives of the bankers, and even the concubines of the personal financiers who funded the Orcanes, may they reign forever, threw out their perfumes. And many ruined perfumers committed suicide. And the others caballed together but even the most ruthless could not bear to assassinate the Flower Maker, addicted as they all were to his art. At last, they hired the most notorious thief of that era, who had assumed the name of Bar Khidr, to steal the Flower Maker's plastic seeds so at least the perfumers could monopolize such poisoned pleasures for themselves.

Now the boss of the city's shurta police had donated two dozen guards to guard the Flower Maker's stock. Besides, the Flower Maker had raised two whining puppicules into enormous dogs.

And the thief, by Fortune's malice, evaded the guards and stole two sacks of seeds but woke the dogs. And the dogs gashed his thighs and rent the sacks, and the guards chased him, limping, into the Suuq of Birds where the food vendors sold sautéed squab to hungry passersby. There he hid in the stalls and let the guards pass, but as he was about to double back he accidentally dropped a seed into a sizzling wok.

And the seed melted and Bar Khidr was felled as even the firmest oaks are felled by the axe of sensuality and inhaled the fumes. What aery parasite the thief inhaled he never knew, only that by burning a single seed he had murdered countless immortal gardens and merited eternal damnation.

And he felt his body rot into compost. And from his compost grew a plastic flower, ravished by the bees of air and darkness. Eight hundred and eighty-eight times this happened. And each time Bar Khidr looked down and saw his roots were fire planted in the gardens of Hell. And the stink of his melting body sickened him. And from his gore arose a man, vomiting through his melting mouth.

And waking briefly from his madness, Bar Khidr fled the city of his birth to the hardscrabble border towns where every night he regrew from his own compost until driven by his visions to enlist with a roving da'i band to fight in the frontier jihad. And we are told he was martyred, by the compassion of god, in front of the walls of Outremer the Damned and at last was tormented no longer by the accursed visions of the Flower Maker.

⊕

The Death of Leibniz's Best of Worlds

> And so Frank Herbert, after debilitating rejections, burned the last manuscript copy of *Dune* in order to devote more time to tripe like the *The Santaroga Barrier.*
> —*American Dictionary of Conjectural Authors*, 4th ed.

⊕

Collateral Nuptialities

> "It was very good of God to let Carlyle and Mrs. Carlyle marry one another and so make only two people miserable instead of four."
> —Samuel Butler

⊕

Etymologically, the word <u>casualty</u> means "being subject to unfortunate chance," in practice "subject to the state of being dead." <u>Collateral</u> then expands the sense to "inexplicable state of being dead."

Etymologically, the word <u>nuptiality</u>, with ligamental letter "i" means "being subject to unfortunate marriage," in practice...well, you get the jab. No need to vaccinate people twice.

Epitaphs and Epishafts

And the child-bride, to honor the World Conqueror who doubtless had been strangled in their private tent by a sectarian assassin, erected 888 mourning towers, one for each of his invincible pubic hairs. Sublime though these remain, down to our pygmied era, they do share one common flaw: At twilight they appear to droop along the shafts, due to a failure to reinforce the foundations in proportion to the softness of the ground.

⊕

Spoiled Milk

"Condemned to starvation in an Akhuan prison, an old man is kept alive by the milk he sucks from the breast of his timid daughter who visits him every night. Caught in the act, the authorities do not put her on trial. In fact, they even feed the old man and rule his death by milk sickness an honorable suicide, so impressed were they by such a selfless love."

Milk Sickness—characterized by severe gastrointestinal distress often leading to death—is thought to be caused by drinking milk from those who have grazed upon the snakeroot plant.

From the "Patchwork Compendium:"

"Diana of Ephesus, with breasts as numerous as the lemons of the lemon tree and enough morphogenetic milk to nourish expectant mothers suffering from amastia, the milk supplies the hormones required to regrow their missing teats until fat and full enough to nurture their babies. Alternatively, a girl not thus afflicted and poisoned by a jealous lover may, by offering her aureoles to Diana, allow the goddess to suck the toxic bile of her entrails out through her breasts."

⊕

Abel Wrath

And Adam preserved the Pre-Adamic Adams and made from them a prayer mat of flesh and kneeling on this he worshipped the Lord Most High and sacrificed their ancestral cutlets.

From Cain came Seth. From Seth came Anosh. From Anosh came Hagar and Kainan. And when Adam died, Seth made a prayer mat of flesh from his adopted father Adam and worshipped. And God showered his blessings on the children of Seth. He multiplied their herds and their harvests and their descendants filled the World and made prayer mats of flesh from their fathers and built cities but fashioned no weapons, trusting in their Lord to defend what He had given.

And Cain, in the 3rd century of the curse, seeing the weakness of Seth and the children of Anosh, took the skin of Abel his brother and tanned it and boiled it in wax made from the choicest portions and glands from Abel's flock and made from this a leather breastplate and a sturdy helm according to the secret method taught to him by the slave girl Lilith in the year of her manumission from Adam.

And Cain recruited the grandchildren of Lilith born from the seed of Harut and Marit, who coupled with the revolutionary daughters of Eve ("and their wombs were as the gates of Hell") and taught them the secrets of sorcery and conspiracy. And Cain went into battle wearing the death mask he had molded from the face of Abel, whose head the angels preserve until the day of wrath. And he made great slaughter of the sons of Seth. Their arrows could not pierce Cain's Abel-hardened armor nor could their stones crush his helm. "And his sigil was the mark of Cain."

And he stretched the hand of dominion across the World.

And God, remembering His promise, hid Hagar from the eyes of Cain. Until the day when the Tribe of Anosh, besieged by Cain and starving, descended from their Spiral Minaret of Hands to betroth Hagar to Cain in exchange for peace. And entering into the betrothal tent, Hagar crushed the skull of the tyrant with the meager leg of her martyred brother Kainan, son of Anosh son of Seth son of Adam, and laid him in the dust of Adam and the pre-Adamic Adams.

CCCCC.Die.XV.

REGISTRVM.

a	iii
b	iii
c	iii
d	iii
e	iii
f	iii
g	iii
h	iii
i	iii
k	iii
l	iii
m	iii
n	iii
o	iii
p	iii
q	iii
r	ii

AN VNPVBLISHED OBITVARY

In his Bustaan, Sa'di saith:
> "It is a crime to give sugar to the sick one,
> For whom, the bitter medicine is fit."
> —H. Wilberforce Clarke

An Vnpublished Obituary

"His moniker meant 'Defender of Men.' A lampoonist might contend that he defended those men he declined to slaughter."

His Life in Monomers

Amiable to hostages.
> Generous with stolen wealth.
> Temperate, relative to the average amount he drank.
> Compassionate towards the widows of his enemies.

The Intended Phenotype or Our Boy Golem

<u>Cleitus</u>: Last of the old guard. Straight-shooter. Alexander preserves and promotes him as propitiation to his father's ghost.

Murdered by way of premeditated rage for reminding his master's son that "with this hand, I saved you at the River Granicus." Alexander grieves and erects a shrine to his newly suspected divinity.

For months Alexander had wondered how best to reward so dangerous a servant. Had Alexander really been a Zoroastrian— the way he pretended to please his Persian sycophants—he might have resided a few millennia in the Aevum, that karmic penalty box, for the cyclical recurrence of his future ancestor Jacob Burckhardt, to find inspiration in Burckhardt's tale of the condottiere who saved the Italian city-state of Siena from invasion. Seeing no way to safely reward him, the city-men said. "Let us kill him and make him our patron saint."

Hephaestion: Nursery-friend. Adjutant. Patroclus to Alexander's Achilles. Like Patroclus, mistaken for Achilles, this time to his benefit. Lame leg, but it is Harpalus who plays the supernal smith. Writes letters to Aristotle, an encrypted history of infamy in contrast to the vedas and veneratiae he shows to his lover. Decryption involves the repeated amputation and prosthesis of letters and blank spaces. The number of transformations required is equal to the months elapsed since the show/trial and execution of Aristotle's nephew Callisthenes multiplied by the thickness, in centidactyls, of the papyrus.

Plautus, in his vulgar way, states that "in their shared tent, Alexander shed his deity to acquire a human penis."

Ptolemy the Vulture: First of the Macedonian elite to accept Alexander as a solar deity, reasoning that the moons, Alexander's subordinates, remain invisible without the sun. Displays a feigned or superstitious reverence for Alexander's corpse. Kidnaps the funeral box on its way to Aegae. Keeps Alexander's liver in a jar. It is said that, afterwards, he never lost a battle until the liver spoiled. We may dismiss as malicious gossip the tale that Ptolemy ate liver slices dipped in honey—like the Cannibal of Uhud, Hind Bint

Utbah, with the Prophet's uncle—to absorb Alexander's latent
genius. His motto, which he steals from Calanus, is that the man
who believes in everything must occasionally believe the truth.

Perdiccas: Likes to send a second messenger to confirm that
the first has not tampered with his orders. Sometimes he sends
contradictory orders to his commanders, to judge which are too
literal-minded and which instinctively submit to his unspoken
will.

Calanus: Ptolemy's Rasputin.

Olympias: Alexander's mother. The Spider Queen. As Richard
the Lion-Heart said of his mother "You are Medea to the teeth,
only this is one son you won't use for vengeance against your
husband..."

Phillip: His father. Assassinated after producing a rival heir.

Eurydice: See Phillip.

The Traitor Bessus: Tied and torn apart by recoiling trees.

⊕

A Vigorous Standing Still

He was what Rumi described. He saw the emptiness within and
filled it with scorpions. He flooded the lovely gardens around the
rim with bleach. After he gutted the world, the cavity called to
him as a craftsman. He built an empire to emphasize the surplus
spaces and rebuilt his friends to suit his empire. The shahid Bar
Yadashr accuses him of forcing his companions to wear the faces
of his Persian victims, Alexander later commands his new Persian
allies to do the same with troublesome Greeks, starting with the
free mercenary companies who opposed him at the River Pinarus.

Unable to conquer the planets, he built glass domes around his cities to fill the sky with reflected conquests.

An Ottoman recension of the Alexander Romance, a collage of anonymous elaborations, tell us that one day Alexander envied the sun. His slaves, out of love, set their master on fire. At the moment of ignition he projected no shadows. Our composite author (collaborating across centuries and cultures) continues. "His flesh smelled like perfume. The body left no ashes to bury."

$\oplus$

The Constitution of Athens

Tradition attributes 158 constitutions to Aristotle. Of those, 38 survived the Macedonian conquest of the Greek city-states. No more than three survived the civil wars which followed Alexander's death. Only one, that of Athens, has come down to us in a doubtful manuscript whose true author may have despised Aristotle.

Alexander's scribes mass-produce constitutional organisms to govern the conquered Greeks, even as Alexander sterilizes their living institutions. In the same way, Phillip of Macedon desiccates Aristotle's birthplace of Stagira[3] then reseeds it with trees of jade. Theophrastus notes that the city's jade citizens shattered, or were misplaced enroute.

$\oplus$

The Spider Queen

"The fungus directs the ant to climb. When the mate arrives to fuck the corpse, the fungus spreads until the mushroom pickers start the cycle fresh again."

$\oplus$

---

[3] Dying in Euboea, Aristotle breathes Mutanabbi's epitaph through the poet's unborn lungs: "The desert, the night, the sword they know me."

Olympias teaches her son writing, horsemanship, the rhetoric
of mass hysteria as counterweight to the "Rhetoric" of his tutor
Aristotle.

Alexander's father Phillip suspected her of being a sorceress.
They rarely shared a bed, but when the moon disrobed he peered
through the keyhole to her room. He never told what he saw, but
his prudent silence suggested ghastly rituals. Orgies, aphrodisiacs
made from the human sigmoid colon, chaplets of plague-ridden
bronze, babbling spider-gods imported from Ifriqiya. The
household slaves said her orb weaver could spin Delphic webs.
Her bindi priestesses would gather up the silk and weave cheerful
destinies, giggling girls who liked to contravene the doom decreed
by the three morbid crones, the Fates—Clothos, Lachesis,
Atropos.

Afterwards, the spiders would ravish the priestesses.

One chamber slave claimed she had seen the queen's
favorite—a sand spider nine inches broad—caress the cheek of its
human bride, as the girl fingered its pedicel.

Aristobolus testifies to Olympias' sense of humor, says that
she liked to wear false legs and crawl over the chests of petrified
serfs.

The most alarming rumor was that every night the royal
baboon spider murdered her, and she was revived or resurrected
by the brown widow's bite.

This domestic malice had an unexpected effect on the
boy Alexander. He developed a fondness for select kinds of
invertebrates though otherwise, as Burckhardt says, "it seemed
that he too, through inborn pride, could no longer regard the low
and crawling things of life."

As for Phillip, he squashed his fear. During the early years of
his reign, these spiders were Phillip's prime assassins. Rebels or
stubborn ambassadors learned to stockpile costly antivenom. Only
when Phillip started taking other wives, wombs for rival heirs, did
spiders crawl into his dreams.

⊕

Wolf Cub Shahada or The Conscious Beast

In the creation of heaven and earth, of tongues and colors, there are signs for those who know.

Of the False Animals. Deceivers, Disclaimers, Declaimers.

The Dagar's feathers spell out the Meccan suras of the Quran. A mangy bird who eats the flesh of men. Its call to salvation is a holy sham.

The rosettes of the leopard of Kerkur, a graceful Naskh calligraphy, delineate a fruitless controversy over eleven hadiths excised by the traditionist Bukhari.

To the partisan crocodile, the Sumatran orangutan reviles Mu'awiyah and extols Ali, both deny the real and fictional existence of the prior three "rightly-guided" caliphs.

The wolf cubs howl their false shahada at the moon. "There is no fire but <u>the</u> Fire." They accuse the sun of stealing from the moon.

The lion—in La Fontaine's fable, he is both Alexander and Alexander's enemy—offers to protect the monkey's treasure from the tiger.

They lie, who say that man is the most treacherous beast.

The Mi'raj and Mirage of Alexander

And Alexander rode the Wheel of Suffering into hell. There, men who resembled him flayed and deboned him, as the saints masturbated to his atonal screams (in concord with the erotic fantasies of the Nasrani Shaykh Tertullian).

At the end of each eternity, the demons and the seraphim host an intramural party. The meat and the guests are Alexander. His inexhaustible blood flows into bottomless tankards. His fat regrows without aid of miracles.

⊕

In unison, the men raised their stones to crush the other Ptolemy, not the Ptolemy who tried to save that Ptolemy who died at Halicarnassus, nor the future dynast and forefather of Cleopatra, but Ptolemy who erected a statue to Gluttony biting her own lips. Ptolemy was now either effacing a life of cowardice by his stoicism or erasing all his heroic deeds by a single act of cowardice. At that moment, Alexander emerged from his tent. The mutiny collapsed, though eight foot soldiers died and a hyspaspist lost his eye before they could restore order.

What had happened was this. The scouts had found a corpse preserved from the bone stripping Samuum beneath his mule, the mule beneath a dune. A Gedrosian deserter or ronin. The man was the spitting image of Alexander.

That had set off the hetairoi, driven by thirst, hallucinations. Their hipparchs insisted that Alexander lived—the real Alexander had gone to scout out a birket kept for thirsty pilgrims—but the hetairoi, suspecting a cover-up, converged on the armory, colliding into a squad of the Companions. In the ensuing brawl, fellowship was discarded. The battle spread, some fighting imaginary Gedrosian infiltrators, others reenacting the River Pinarus where they had crushed the first slave army of Darius.

And why had Alexander failed to show himself? Was it because of this—returning as the mutiny began—that one of the loyalist hetairoi had ridden right over him, mistaking him for a mutineer in the chaos (his commander sentenced the guilty rider to death, but Alexander commuted the sentence to 20 lashes and then promoted him)? Or, as Quintus Curtius suspects, had Alexander's agents incited the mutiny to flush out the malcontents who had been planning a wider insurrection? Curiously, the cynical Curtius fails to perfect his conspiracy theory by accusing Alexander of planting the body double.

He tread on spiderwebs. He had broken the mutiny, but these were wolves not dogs. They prowled. They clumped like blood, babbling now, but from culverts Alexander heard the underpop

and shisk of knives, the snick of spear points cresting sand, the
baridrone of smothered rage. As in war, when a phalanx cracks
but does not shatter, fleeing but still organized enough to rally
and return to the fight or instead to trample their own allies. Not
individual choice but mob momentum would decide. A single man
could tip the avalanche.

He must preempt that man.

He urged them not to defeat themselves when salvation was
close at hand. The coast was not far. He'd received a messenger
from his navarch Nearchus (duly, a letter was produced which
seemed authentic) which assured them three hard days of
marching. No more.

He recounted their victories, more glorious than Marathon or
Salamis. What were those? Minor skirmishes, puppets shedding
puppet blood. They had killed a god, avenged Persian atrocities
against the Greeks, freed the enslaved peoples of the world.

He mourned their losses in this disastrous retreat through
Gedrosia. He named each fallen soldier, slave and horse by name,
a testament to his perfect memory. And by a rhetorical swerve he
had learned from Aristotle, transformed these losses into evidence
of their invincibility. Helios himself had taken the field. Only
the Sun, beyond the range of their slings, could stand against a
Macedonian.

He spoke all night, out in the open air, as his troops hid
beneath an outcropping, taught by hard experience to flee the
sadist star.

Seeing how parched he was, Zephyrus brought him a helmet
full of water, which Alexander contemptuously poured on the
ground. That did the trick. Even the veterans began crying.
Prudently, they drank their tears. The mutineers confessed with
such pathetic zeal that Alexander, trusting to Fortune, pardoned
all but the ringleaders, who were cut to pieces by their former
confederates.

Presently, Alexander fainted and had to be carried back to his
tent, though he sent Perdiccas at intervals to reassure the men.

The Myth of Er

His wound was festering. The fever struck. This time he dreamt
he murdered his other selves, broke the Wheel of Incarnation to
become the dreamshape of his choice, ascending in defiance of
mutation canon law, from worm to flower to butterfly to storm,
from thunder dogs whining to puppicules up to the helium of
the magnetosphere to the asteroid belt, his body dividing into the
dust of Andromeda, the grains dividing into those atoms which so
horrified Democritus. So high he could look down on the gods.
He could just pick out his mother Olympias weaving her webs
around the other supernal spiderettes. Below them crawled the
race of Man, infernal ants, organic war machines who make the
bloody-handed gods appear compassionate.

With that same celestial eye, he scanned the Gedrosian waste,
whose skinless hills might yet entomb his routed armies.

Wrath, a sudden madness, took him.

His undreaming shell raved so harshly that the slave-girl
pressed the wet cloth to his brow harder than protocol allowed.

Alexander moaned. Had they died? The deserters who
would deny our cookpots out of spite and feed their flesh to
desert birds. The wounded we have abandoned to drink their
own blood and seal each other's eyes with frozen tears. The last
to die will guide the resurrected blind across the river Lethe. The
Macedonian boast is that we (even the nullipedes, pus-feeding
amputees) will spit on the boatman and swim across as a single
unit.

Or might they live?

In 200 years, our descendants may encounter theirs. Overrate
ourselves as great explorers. Mistake each other for savages.
Slaughter them, as Odysseus is said to have killed the castaway
Ithacans, parents of his forgotten parents, on his homeward

voyage. Besiege their cities until starving neighbors exchange their children, grieving less to grind unbeloved bones to flour. Hypnos-eyed Laestrygonians who eat unnatural flesh that men died to look upon.

The Glorious

The augurs, twice interrogated, replied the words of Oedipus the King.

Alexander feared a pathetic end. To defy this adverse augury, he tried to die as Achilles did. At every opportunity he tried. His own victories appalled him. They increased the chance of illness, old age, a pathetic accident. He must die in battle. Cut down, shot, drowned, disemboweled. Or vaporized by foreign gods.

In Egypt, he adopted himself as the son of Amun hoping that if the god did not himself exist, then his angry devotees would tear him apart.

He snuffed out the Seven Unburning Fires of Ahura Mazda. The lofty, the fertile, the compassionate, the beneficent, the defender, the bountiful, the hearth lord. He crowned himself the Persian Sun. He slept outside, beneath the sadist-star, its vengeful sprays sizzled harmless off his armor.

He substituted himself for the lead actor in the roving theatre that trailed his invading armies and wore the Alexander mask in reenactments of the River Pinarus and Guagamela. He hoped these arrogant attempts to repeat his own godlike victories would invite nemesis and destruction.

Once, he ran naked into the forest but for his rams-head helmet. He clothed himself in mud and moss. He darted with the sacred fawn. Hoping that Diana the Huntress might peg an arrow between his horns.

⊕

The Beloved Murshid or The Vndesired One

Was it the saddlebag or his hand trembling? Alexander had not taken Hephaestion into his bed for many years, but here was the apeirogon,[4] the lover's cryptogram.

How its chiralets, coruscending conduits of braided parasites, dragged the eye. How it shattered the present mind, to reunify flawed continents of memory.

He felt the kisses, their first wrestling match, the musk from fractured pearl drops of sweat, the degrading busy work, the rearguard commands and sinecures to deflect charges of favoritism, the adulteries demanded by policy, the other adulteries, the make-up sex, Alexander's habit of twisting left in sleep to thrust his arm through the leather strap lest to grip the pike he drop his shield.

Alexander, le petit morts, reading Plato while humming in chocolate baritone those Lydian harmonies that Plato despised as fatal to the state. As he sang, he improvised lyrics from the Myth of Er, reincarnating dead Persian heroes—Jamshyd, Rustam, Kaikobad—as conscripts in the Macedonian army.

False memories. The misremembering of true memories.

Alexander's broken leg, bits of bone sticking to the folds of Hephaestion's ceremonial chiton. The charging mare, trained to

---

[4] A polygon which tries to be a sphere but disappoints.

The theogony of the apeirogon is uncertain. The heresiarch Bar Huthayl, on the very steps to the guillotine, worshipped it as a demiurge. Bar Hudayj contends that it existed pre-eternally with the First.

The Akhuans tell us that it was harvested from the hair ("pubic hairs" claims Bar Khidr, our latter-day De Sade) of Penelope, widow of Odysseus. Who, to give a theme to her mourning tapestry and to delay her suitors, spins the tale of her own chicanery. In doing so, she accidentally encompasses all may or may-not histories.

The gullible reiterate that the tapestry repeats perfectly (may The Inscrutable hide us from false opinions). In truth, it is saved from such blasphemy by the subtle errors introduced by human frailty into otherwise redundant scenes.

trample fallen enemies, driven mad by a peacock from Phillip's menagerie.

(Unborn horses driven mad. The horse-repellent elephant charge, their feet like celestial battering rams.)

The close escape. How in a sunken chamber, a megaron or a cenote, they renewed childish vows, annually, with oxen gore, each owed their survival to some guiding jinn (or genius) of the other. The limping lavish boy who roused the roosting royal tailor from his harem to hem a fresh chiton so Hephaestion would not disgrace himself at the feast.

Cardamom coffee in India. Burnt lip. The coolness of his lip sucking his.

Exile, when the plot against Alexander's father fails. The sheltered bay, the islands winking in and out of fog, the orgiastic hills, epic scenery. Despair with no epic deeds to do, no <u>arete</u>, no pursuit of excellence.

The clouds rolling like beheaded kings. The blushing sky, the sky in black mourning for the ruined East.

Phillip's funeral. The spasmodic death of Caranus, Phillip's heir alternate, and Alexander's erudite dinner talk with a notorious poisonologist of cordials masked by Argive wine, toxic ink, a camphor rubbed on Cretan boar. Hephaestion, the first and only one to drain his cup.

The time Alexander made him eat fake grapes, like Erigone who sold her virginity to Dionysus for the same.[5] Were all his gifts counterfeit? Alexander knew it didn't matter. Hephaestion would treasure the fakes the way he ate those grapes, with premeditated gullibility.

Hephaestion remembered the taste of wax, his rage the second time he recalled that taste. How he later regretted that remembered rage, his grief when, sun-struck on a crag in the

---

[5] As a joke, Dionysus teaches her unsuspecting father, Icarius, the fermenter's art. Icarius shares his primeval wine with shepherds. They think he has poisoned them, kill him, then bury him in penitence. The family dog, led by excessive love, unearths the body. Erigone hangs herself.

Gedrosian desert, he could not remember what he regretted or why he raged. The sun is skinning him, but he shivers, decrepit, in soldier years at least and cold, like a volcano puffing ersatz steam.

Three times, Alexander had passed him figs and said, "A side-dish for a side-dish." His way of saying, "Tonight, I'm fucking someone else."

Sometimes, Alexander said, "I made you from a dream."

Sweet sophistic solipsisms.

Sometimes, he said, "I dreamt, and when I woke, you were my dream's sweet residue."

Sedulous sentiments.

And once, aping their tutor Aristotle, "Achilles loves all Patrocles...Hephaestion is a Patroclus. Therefore..."

A suspect syllogism.

Hephaestion is walking now. He does not know when he leapt off his horse. Perhaps he fell off. There's a nasty splotch across his thigh, as when gods scrape the battlefield clean of human bugs.

He sinks again into other Hephaestions.

By the time he emerges, Alexander is already inside of him. After he finishes, it is Hephaestion who wraps his ankles around Alexander's legs and will not let him pull out. This pain, too, is the only pleasure Alexander has given him in many years.

Three weeks later, Hephaestion dies.

For 18 years, Alexander had shielded him from the plots of jealous sycophants and resentful chiliarchs. This solicitude preserves Hephaestion long enough to die of pneumonia.

Alexander had loved him. Politically, it was safer to abuse him and once abused, to abuse again. His Persian pretensions had distracted him. The conflation of the Greek Helios with the unburning Persian Fire demanded careful massaging of Persian brides and Persian mobs, as well as intricate negotiations with Persian priests (and their conniving interpreters). Two delusory civilizations, Greek and Persian, had slaughtered each other. He would fuse them into a single organism.

Alexander mandates monthly sacrifices to his lover. This relieves his rivals. A jumped-up catamite is dangerous, a god is bribeable. Sometimes after a bloody day Alexander forgets, but then he sacrifices twice as many bulls at dawn and pours libations to the gods of Dis, the tri-caste milk of burnt Persepolis: honey, olive oil and Indian butter.

Alexander carves ayats into Hephaestion's funeral box, cast from the unused gold of Phillip's coffin and clad in red ram skins. The box is lost in the power struggles which follow Alexander's death. The traditionists claim that Ptolemy had the verses recarved to strengthen his claim as Alexander's prime intimate.

Fourteen centuries pass. A more convincing Persian, Hafiz, supplies those words defaced by time or ambition.

> The anka,
> Our pure existence,
> Is the prey of none.
> The teeth of the snare cannot pierce
> Our enmeshing skin.
> Known of name, unknown of body.
> Achilles drank the wine and Patroclus
> Drank Achilles-blood.
>
> I have run thirty years in unity
> And thirty more in singularity
> And still I have not reached
> The Desired One.

The Pursuit of Excellence

Meanwhile...back in Thebes.

Editorial page, *The Daily Hellene*, Summer Solstice issue, the 12th Boedromion, "On the Importation of Persian Institutions, Notably the Social Synod, Into the Prostrate Peloponnese."

"The Social Synod is an amalgamation of city-states. An abomination, a barbarian invention. The pollution of the polis. The death of the Republic.

"The Social Synod is the erasure of human beings in favor of illusional tendencies. It is a particle dividing to nothingness, a paper trail of invisible ink, a burning database.

"The gods have afflicted us.

"In the Social Synod every man is a spy. You can't help but spy. Every day you witness so many actions that one or two must be crimes.

"No man commits great deeds. There are no deeds, no <u>arete</u>, no pursuit of excellence. No pursuit. The best you can hope is to add momentum to the Mass (that imploding supernova of the Mob).

"No less certain. All deaths are anonymous. Your heroic, your cowardly deeds are crushed in an avalanche of averages. Statistically your virtue tends towards nullity. Percentage-wise you do not exist. The percentage is the only organism proven to exist. If abstractly it is insisted that you—the "you" that is now only a crankish conspiracy theory—might still influence reality as statistical noise, an index of weighted whimpering, a trend, or cultural <u>disposition</u>, that "you" will soon be annihilated by social abjurements and seasonal revisions."

⊕

Six Dreams of a Third

I read in Burckhardt that Petrarch kept a Greek copy of *The Iliad* which he could not understand. But he prayed to it in Italian.

This head-grown story comes (erupts) from that fortuitous reading.

⊕

Alexander thought he slept, free from the bedlam of the camp. Silence and a missing lump woke him up.

A void (which abhors philosophers) had coagulated beneath his pillow. Six hours earlier, the pillow had clutched the head of Darius—bygone god of Persia, Hind and Babylon—as though his neck had worn a crown of flesh. In math of conquests won, 600 years had passed, the time it took the Achaemenids to build what Darius had just pissed away in a single battle.[6] A triumph which 6,000 years of human cant and catastrophe would not efface.

But these were computations for other insomnias. Frantic, Alexander could not find his copy of *The Iliad*, emended by his boyhood tutor Aristotle to emphasize, in ways that Homer had carelessly omitted, the affinity between Alexander and Achilles—the man of wrath.

Too exhausted to fully wake, too dismayed to rest, at last Alexander collapsed. So many burdens. So much to plan. They had crushed the Persian army. The traitor Bessus had done his work. Now they must hunt him down. Policy demanded that Alexander avenge the sacrilege done to a fellow king.

And then...his new Persian constituency demanded dangerous ideas. If he wanted to rebuild a reich, not just an empire, he must reconcile the Barbarian to the Greek. He would make a new gestation, or a suicide that would elevate his life to art.

And so he slept. With growing confidence that his retinue had, at worst, mislaid the scroll with the tent's other baggage. In this tent Alexander slept to symbolize his dominance. A political not personal insult, his legendary courtesy to the Persian queen already prefigured medieval fantasies of chivalric love.

Two conflicting dreams.

In the first, Hephaestion sends Alexander's cup boy to return the scroll.

In the second, the boy has just stolen it. As he runs, he transforms into Agamemnon stealing Briseis, the Trojan-war-prize girl of Achilles. Alexander throws his javelin.

A brief anecdote in Quintus Curtius tells us that a cup boy of a similar name dies months later of stomach pains which

---

[6] Herodotus may inflate the antiquity of the Persian dynasties.

Alexander's chiliarchs attribute to accidental ingestion of poison
and an amateurish poisoner. The Roman annalist attributes
this anecdote to a lost history of Callisthenes who overhears
Alexander relating the hostile dreams to Ptolemy. To which
Ptolemy exclaims that even Alexander's nightmares "change their
predestined shape" to soothe his fears.

In the second dream, the javelin pins the boy to the door
of Babylonian oak. Later, the servants clean grease and gore.
They tell Alexander that his cup boy had died two weeks ago
of rheumatic fever and that Perdiccas had delivered the missing
Iliad to the wrong tent. Alexander accepts this story, afraid to
investigate.

Only when the first two dreams have killed themselves will
Alexander wake up from the third (the fourth dream will be his
ephemeral empire). Then he will recall that he had lost his copy
of *The Iliad* months ago, in the pyre which his dancing girls had
made of Persepolis, that less immortal Troy. That night the girls
had been his ravagers and may have included a Helen and a Helen
clone.

⊕

Ethics of the Baryon

Alexander ejects our modern sociology from his mind. The idea
that <u>being</u> matters more than <u>doing</u> was anathema. A good Greek,
he worshipped verbs. He would be the first to tell you that "should
Alexander ever stop moving, he would disappear."

⊕

The Moon Before the Sun

The document read:

"...the theologians have proven more agreeable than the
priests. They posit that the ancestral sunburst of our Argead
royal dynasty—which, on the sound advice of [redacted] we have

readopted—is identical to the emblem of Ahura Mazda, the pre-eternal fuel of the Unburning Fire. Their certainty is requested." Here, the word <u>requested</u> has been scratched out in a rheumatic hand and replaced with <u>required</u>. The sparse bureaucratic style of the letter could have belonged to any of a hundred court eunuchs or fiscal scribes.

Perdiccas picked at the royal seal. He knew that etched chrysolite was impossible to forge, yet he suspected that were he to tattoo Alexander's orders across his chest, his own men would skin him alive.

For the third time, he dropped the scroll and turned to the letter. <u>The</u> letter, from the Stagirite. As he read it, he felt his heart flicker like a senile star. His hands trembled as though diffusing into mist.

He lost his nerve and turned to his own half-finished letter.

"To Ptolemy. A proposal."

He had struggled all evening to address his rival in the proper tone, to avoid both a suspicious humility or overt contempt.

At last, he abandoned all subtlety. Alexander was going insane. In the streets, the people proclaimed that the Saoshyant, the Persian Messiah had risen in the West. The time for reason was past, they had to shatter him...

"...he commands his satraps, in the absence of their god-king, to greet all foreign ambassadors in darkness. Total darkness! The same applies to the weekly court. Even as we pronounce our judgments in blindness, we are now required to wear a dappling moon of brass to symbolize that we are no more than the fetal irradiance of his aboriginal star."

"As though proskynesis was not enough! I had to disarm the men and lock the armory and still I barely kept them from mutiny, and I tell you now that they prostrated themselves with their daggers wet. Now he wants to rename his horse to Pegasus who Carries the Sun. One of the eunuchs—I think that popinjay, Phanes—planted <u>that</u> idea. A minor disaster by comparison.

"Our function, as exarchs, is to consent. Our duty is
to interpret orders as patriotically as we dare. I await your
interpretations." He sealed the letter and sent the guard to fetch
the courier. He wondered how much Ptolemy had offered the man
to turn on him, how hard he had considered it. Gods below, he
did not have enough men to both spy on Ptolemy <u>and</u> to spy on
Ptolemy's agents in his own camp.

That menial fiend. Now more than ever, he needed to know
Ptolemy's plans. He had exaggerated the mutinous temper of his
men (gods above, at least it might plant the seed of hubris in the
bastard's head) and sacrificed twin peregrines to Tyche for luck in
deception, and inscribed a curse upon the sacral tablet: "Let ants
eat his eyes, his organs dissolve in acid. Let me destroy the silk
houses of this caddis-fly, the traps and decoys he has devised. Let
the traps engulf the trap maker."

⊕

The Wedge in the Wheel

In the early days of the Alexander cult in India there was a
dearth of trained da'is to spread the word, so the traveling pandal
came into vogue. The call went out. Famous sculptors and
miniaturists would compete for a commission to decorate these
folding skin boxes with relief carvings or painted panels. The
medium was mottled flesh stretched and mounted on teak or
rosewood.

Hirelings could operate the pandal with little training and no
understanding what the stories were about, though a pujari was
assigned, when available, to answer simple riddles posed by the
audience.

The inner flaps were to depict the Core Mysteries and were
locked against the uninitiated. The outer flaps were devoted
to low-minder art, capricco genre tales or popular moral fables
centered around famous battles or instructive episodes.

Among the most illustrious of these:

There is Alexander shooting the Dagar Bird as it perfidiously venerates the Simurgh, the bird who is and is in all birds.

The siege and sack of Aornus, which even the god Krishna had failed to conquer. Alexander's victory is one of the talismans or signs of his Deity.

The admonishment of Dandamis that Alexander had conquered nothing but dirt in which to bury himself.

There is that anecdote that Mencken attributes to Ambrose Bierce of wives guarding the crematorium fires to make sure their husbands did not escape. There is that pandal which depicts Macedonian soldiers burning wooden boxes for warmth during a winter siege. Later they found that the boxes were coffins encrypting husbands of the besieged. Perhaps their wives, trapped in that starving town, breathed a sigh of relief.

Finally, there is the Retribution Cycle which begins with the Great King's invasion of Greece and ends at the River Pinarus where Alexander's armies slay so many Persians that they clog the cog of suffering. And it is true that Alexander's wars produce more corpses than the Cog can grind and reincarnate. There is a modern-day sect whose devotees blame the cumulative effects of this brief malfunction for the present fertility crisis.

Cf. the satirical "Wheel of Salvation" by the Saksiwa philosopher Tomayashi, where the backlog produces redundant messiahs. Each begins his preaching before the prior incarnation has had a chance to die on the cross, leading to an infinite loop of messianic coup and countercoup.

The Golden Child

He was the Golden Child of an unreal god.

His cult of molecular suicide arose in Hastinapura, in the former empire of Gandhara. Only when human beings learned to nurture death, to leave no monomer, no residue for rebirth, would they break the cycle of suffering.

Thousands quit their jobs, abandoned father/mother/bride, left their crops to rot in the field, made pyres of their monks and wisdom books, refused to pay their taxes and stoned Alexander's army recruiters to death.

The Golden Child's devotees soon compounded satraps, serfs and fiscal scribes, generals, import-export kings, astrologers and those less wise

One famous convert was Ptolemy.

Every night—twice at dawn—he took up the clay tablet and the stylus which still bears the name of the Imposter, knelt before the master, undressed his heart, recited the lessons, hearing the voice—that voice, which the ulema assert, first spoke the suras of the uncreated Quran, predating language, body language, bodies and time.

In the morning, Ptolemy would prostrate himself, that the pilgrims arriving to transfigure themselves might use his hair to lap up blood.

At noon, the child—whose body reeked of open sores, whose untreated cuts had grown gangrenous—would die as parsimoniously and didactically as he could to edify the crowd.

Afternoons, Ptolemy would curate death. He starved until his stomach began to eat itself. He remodeled his own body according to the eight-fold path—skinning, erosion, excision, incision, resection, contortion, constriction, lyes. He broke his bones and encased himself in molds. He slept with lepers. He wrapped himself around wire frames until his tendons tore, wore vesicular diadems and rings of belly fat and when the knives grew dull, plowed furrows with his fingernails.

And when he had surpassed the child in adroit suicide, the unreal god—Our Lord of Nullity reified, concretized—came into being and manifested himself to Ptolemy. From this revelation, Ptolemy produced supplemental Anatomies and reviled the Golden Child in the weekly Synod as a gnostic, an obscurantist, an egoist who had withheld these Subdermal Sutras (those of wasting diseases, supernal acids, the nine corrosive eczemas) from his disciples out of overweening pride.

Enraged, his dearest acolytes bound the Golden Child in chains and buried him alive to deny salvation to his accursed bones. Against this, Aristobolus claims that they, moved by a lingering compassion, threw the child into a vat of aqua regia, the only primitive acid which could dissolve gold.

Hundreds died in the ensuing schism. Alexander hunted down the rest. A remnant fled into the mountains, but without new members to replenish their numbers, they soon died out in the normal practice of their religion.

By then Ptolemy had apostatized and returned to Alexander, mission accomplished.

On the Generation...

Alexander's armies had diverted the rivers. The traitors died of thirst but so had the hellebore fields, though his botanists[7] preserved a single specimen. He had not thought of his tutor in years, but the flower which he had made unique reminded him of that unclonable mind and of his own secret failure.

Reclining in his tent, Alexander tips the capsa with his toe, pulls out the scroll and reads Aristotle's admonition aloud, with the inflection of a man who has often staked his salvation on a single speech, "But Nature flies from the infinite, for the infinite is unending or imperfect and Nature ever seeks an end."

Of Conspiracies

In Babylon, the number of classified documents grew beyond an immortal archivist's ability to catalogue. Derived from Assyrian numerology, the Macedonian ciphers are so sophisticated that they appear as unencrypted Greek, to the point they fool

---

[7] Slaves, in fact, the world's first and only botanist had declined to follow the victorious armies.

Alexander's own cryptographers, who accidentally decrypt thousands of embarrassing letters, among them the covert negotiations with Bessus to betray Darius, and an order to suppress the investigation into the drowning of Perdiccas.

Of Phantasmions

Reliable witnesses inform him of young and invasive empires, arable secessionists sprouting throughout his Empire, ever triumphant, enslaving his citizens, massacring his garrisons. But his scouts fail to uncover these upstart emperors, the mass graves, or the witnesses. In despair, his scouts fabricate troop counts, census rolls, topographies, flora, fauna, mills, treasuries, taboos, temples, blasphemies. They even pose as ambassadors from these real or fabulous confederacies to delay Alexander's wrath.

Of Enemies

To conquer India, he must take Kashmir. To take Kashmir, he must smash the Punjab and the unassailable fortress of Aornus. To hold Aornus, he must control the vast Hindu Kush. To control the Hindu Kush, he must conquer India—then, as now, a vortex of fractured powers.

It takes so long to travel from kingdom to kingdom that his most craven puppet-governors forget Alexander's face, the insignia of the Argead House, even his ethnicity. So much that two Vedic tribes, the Taxsas and the Tugras, who had hailed him as their liberator from Persian rule, attack him as he retires from his "victories" in Sind, not recognizing the ragged prodigal of so many ruined armies.

Unwilling to dare the fathomless Hyphasis River, his demoralized army had mutinied a thousand miles from what the Greek geographers presumed to be the end of the world. They who had boasted they would spit on the boatman and swim across the river Lethe as a single unit had been broken by a single elephant charge.[8]

Zeno's paradox. They can move no farther. Alexander can never catch up to his own legend. Before he can kill <u>all</u> his enemies, he must kill half that number. To kill half, he must first kill a quarter. At last he cuts a single man to pieces. He cuts each piece to pieces. From this fission spills the indivisible baryons which so horrified Democritus.

Of Heroism

"The bee who only pollinates the tallest flowers, exhausted, comes crashing down to earth."

His epic grows so long that the bards, by custom compelled to embellish rather than invent original songs, grow hoarse before they can reach their own embellishments.

They might have saved their voices by recrooning the same murder 8,888 times. Alexander has killed so many people that in the future he will kill, if not literal clones, a genetic rehash of his past victims.

Of Happiness

Or how he atones.

He scours the casualty reports for the amputation of redundant limbs.

---

[8] In the battle against the Elephant-Lord Porus, two hetaroi see a white elephant, the ghost of that which ancient Rustam slew. It shatters the Macedonian center and almost tramples Alexander, whom his Persian conscripts had taken to calling the Son of Rustam. Alexander's fabulists, taking full advantage, had incorporated that hero into Alexander's demigodly genealogy, however much the Persian paladin clashed with Amun, Heracles, the kinslayer Arjuna and other useful forefathers.

He seeks barren brides. He appoints incompetent obstetricians.

He spends all his time with eunuchs. He instructs his gardener to clip the reproductive stamens of all the Hanging Flowers of Babylon.

He massacres a sect of dasturs who preach the redundant judgment of Ahura Mazda, who repeatedly clones and sends all copies to Hell.

He cannot end nor make an end.

He buries himself in the palace of Babylon, a labyrinth of diminishing courtyards, gardens, odalisques. He buries his head in the lap of the Divine Roxanne. To distract himself, he reads aloud the letters of Aristophanes which Harpalus has kindly or perfidiously sent to him. Aristophanes' second letter to Sellos strikes him as perverse, outlining the comic dramatist's solution to the priggish ending of Aeschylus' "Eumenides." In Aristophanes' version, rather than placate the Furies or submit to the arbitration of Athena, Orestes ingests a certain flower and forgets that he is his mother's murderer. He transforms himself into a guiltless man, if not wholly innocent.

Alexander recalls that flower. Of the several species of hellebore, there is only one, baladhur, whose sepals clutch its bud in the way Aristophanes describes. His botanists had gotten it wrong.

Ingested, baladhur annihilates undesired memories. He had only to revile his tutor. Proper preparation required an expert hand. He sent for Calanus, Ptolemy's herbalist and intimate.

His slaves find him with a knife in his heart, fingers covered in correction powder. An unfinished letter to Antipater lays beside him, instructing his regent to execute Aristotle. Beneath that lies a second letter addressed to Aristotle. Entire paragraphs have been rubbed out. The missing term of his refutation had eluded him all night. Even had he justified himself, he would have forgotten his victory.

THE GIRLS GVIDE TO GHOST FVCKING

An obligatory warning before we begin, brought to you by the Society for the Suppression of Supernatural Vice:

From Sextus Empiricus we learn that sensation is change, to change is to be mortal, to feel is to die, therefore, the damned cannot feel, they burn without pain, uncold and unwarm, infinite infants, senile immortals, father-mother and child, they give birth to themselves. In the same way that Hafiz—in his mystic fuck poems (ghrazal, sultry-sacred diminuendo)—breeds roses, wine, cryptoerotic mountebanks, neophyte doms, every molecule and moon (the moon too is a molecule), a slot-and-slut machine of mispronounced or misspelled amino embryons that somehow reproduce a genomic dipygus named Hafiz. There is no distinction but what our arrogance or madness compels.

Now given all that, girls, what's the point of trying to fuck a ghost?

Every ghost is damned. The Damned are eternal. For them, counting and time are unthinkable. Thinking is unthinkable. Thinking about time takes time (the time to zip from neuron to neuron, but the distance between ghost neurons is the distance from Archduke Franz Ferdinand to Emperor Palpatine (or Leopardi's "Mother of the Eucharist" from "Sunday Candy")). Ergo, ghosts are stupid, however much of a cunnilingual crackerjack they may be in a munch.

And get used to topping.

Or sub-topping or bottoming for a demi-dumb-dom. Ghosts don't act. They react—inconclusively.

Ghosts are generic. You're specific, with a specific body chemistry, you-do-you stimulants, a mensurable chonkitude and proud of it. Ghosts (here the Neoplatonists converge on postmodern biology) are airy, anorexic oxygen, abstract, a rom-com drizzle-down in a CGI hurricane. Ghosts fuck democratically but have never yet fucked a specific constituency. They gift diffusively, sport hazy, scattershot hard-ons for Humanity. They are perpetually infecting and being infected (though, again, inconclusively) with STDs. And while a little gris-gris in the pee-pee is no reason to panic, the risk of viral transmission from eternity to temporality deserves systematic study.

Every ghost is damned.

Sure, being damned does give them that goth-core-dank-OG-vegan-vampire-cosplay-lo-pan-steampunk-ragazza-baccazza-homeless-hipster with a dark past appeal. There's the fact that ghosts don't change so you're never tempted to change them. And yes, that chiseled chest (like anabolic ice), that gelid smile, those brooding tits and ghastly gams could outlast the Laocoön Group and most museum catalogues. You like dad-bods? That dad-bod's gonna stay a dad-bod from Eve's First Brunch (the apocryphal Adamic Grand Opening) to the biocidal degringolade of the poly-cellular borganism. And as long as they died at least "half-mast" (see Tip#1 below) they're pretty much randy to go, at least until their penitential promissory notes are paid down. I have yet to encounter Ghost-Cialis on WebMD.

I'll be in my bunk.

Just kidding?

Anyways, now that we've about flatlined our legal team, here are eleven supernal—or infernal—tips for novice ghost fuckers which are guaranteed to help me feed my kids this month.

1. Make sure your trick died *in flagrante delicto*.

This rule is a double down if they lean male as incremental erections (perpetually erecting at the generational pace of a cathedral) are possible, but patience unto Mother Teresahood is key. Otherwise, sans rod, lube helps. The key word here is "helps." Don't expect to transform their Dune Planet into Splooshtown over anything less than ecological timescales.

2. Text over talk.

"The time to talk to fish is when they're on the hook."

In practice, though, your bon-rio-onryo is prone to bitch and moan sepuchrally on the best days. If you insist on face to "face" communication, brush up on body language. Don't try to project a poker face onto a shuffling poker deck and <u>don't</u> paint a definite emotion over that pentimento-collage of mouths and eyebrows, museum of past and maybe-molecules.

3. Test the waters.

Whale out some sexy sonar. Give them time to visualize their kinks, preferably post-coital and over a strategic text session on their Didi ride home (see #2). Don't act anything out. Not yet. The VR can be hotter than the act, and this gives you a chance to frame your own kinks as free-trade or, alternatively, to keep some of your rancid buttered pecan, sotto voce, between you and our cunni-lingual comrades over at the "Do It Better Column" here at *Impresario Kerkur*. Pushing too hard for reciprocity can put a caperture on your aperture in short order.

4. A geas today is ED (erectile dysfunction) tomorrow.

Hark to Dr. Burckhardt when he states "A curse is a mix of hate and impotence." Encourage them to seek paracultic intervention for their own peace of mind. Don't shame. But if that cross on their back is the only wood they're carrying, dump them. A basic martyr is only slightly less <u>grating</u> (*face-palm emoji) than a cheddagogue whining about suboptimal wine pairings.

5. Just because he's dragging around all those chains...

Doesn't mean he's GGG.

6. Respect the gag-reflex of innocent bystanders.

He or she may be your tortured tater-tot or ottering-ostrus,[9] you may be their chonky cotoroanţă calembour. But your slobbering, ectoplasmic kisses are arousing bivalve bowel eruptions, not jealousy.

7. Don't sacrifice friends and family.

Seriously. Don't do it. You'll thank yourself for the support network later. Besides, guts for guts and dermal to dermal, the viscera exchange rates suck and have been getting worse in recent centuries. At best, mulching your sister might buy you a patch the size of your best friend Clarissa's trashy foot tattoo. Tipping an extra racist uncle or two could regenerate enough of a lung and vocal cords for your trick to gutter out a passable "thank you." But without a functioning circulatory system, gangrene pretty much sets in immediately. And no one likes a kinslayer.

8. Brie-breeze (or stank dick). It's a thing.

Ghost douching is not (also, no sugaring—sorry follicle-phobes, it's a physics thing). Whatever hygienic state, or expiration date they were in post-compost-mentis, that's how they're going to stay. But do take the long view. Ghosts don't sweat or fart. As to bad breath, it's never getting worse, if never mint fresh.

---

[9] Not to be confused with the *Oestrus*, or domesticated pussy parcher, a creature of asymmetric kinks and predilections, whose sexual statecraft can be difficult to distinguish from its puritanical ratonnades. Its tedious irrumations may induce dithering ovulations followed by a cooldown period (the gynecological "rovinava") of penitential celibacy.

9. Never reenact the tragic circumstances surrounding their death.

If we have to explain this one, you're fucked but not fucking, a sad *état de choses* (say it in a faux French accent, who else would compare a human orgasm to "the little death"?)

10. Practice safe sex.

A motherly PSA.

Ghosts reproduce like hippity-hoppity (no, not Tupac) holograms.

Birth control. Curse control. Just because there's no penetration doesn't mean that <u>interpenetration</u> is risk free. Yes, the classic full-body condom from *The Naked Gun* is a joke. But a sturdy pullover and rain boots could save you an expensive course of astral antibiotics and be a hell-baby saver too.

11. Get used to extremes.

Too thin. Too thick. Paranormal porridge dick is hard to find among more terrestrial offerings.

⊕

To sum up. You're fucked if you do. Definitely not fucked if you don't. So you do you. You have only yourselves to damn.

⊕

Dear Reader. We need your support...

There's changing your creed to agree with the world. And changing the world to agree with the creed.

Our only creed—our antique sacrament—here at the *Impresario Kerkur* is "tip generously (Patreon link below) and subscribe."

THE IDOL OF ENOCH

In the same way Aesculapius, when Enoch had died, erected an idol to his tutor in the Temple of the Lord. Every morning—twice in the afternoon—the prince of the Sphere the Core of the World, took up the clay tablet and the stylus, which still bear the name of the Imposter, knelt before the master, undressed his heart, recited the lessons, hearing the Voice—that voice, which the ulema assert first spoke the suras of the uncreated Quran, predating language, body language, bodies, and time.

Men hedged their bets. They prayed to god, but Enoch they worshipped, though he heard no prayers but that of his prime disciple. For Aesculapius dogfully executed Enoch's unspeakable will, rewarding the pious and destroying the kafirs in the here and now, leaving no monomer, no molecule for the fire below.[10] The fate of the damned was no less horrible than the joy of the blessed. The damned were digested in gastric prisons. The redeemed were

---

[10] Bar Shibli writes that on the Day of Judgment "the Tree will rise from the Garden of Hell, its branches impale every kafir in the world, for monstrously it grows, though its roots are fire." Bar Juhani, to deflect accusations that this implacable growth represents an unjust predestination, interprets this as an allegory for the man who impales himself on his own self-consuming pride. Like Dante, he could not abandon his beloved pagans to eternal torment for the accidental sin of dying centuries before the message of salvation. Out of pity, he denies an unchanging judge who cannot change his mind.

consigned to numinous worlds where sunrise darkens the sky and hunger is a crime.[11]

His enemies whispered that Aesculapius so adored the idol that he would rather have been[12] the idol than alive. Bar Hebraeus calls Aesculapius the father of idolatry. Bint Halima calls him "father to idols." An infamous scribal error will render this as "fathering gods," giving rise to heterodox traditions[13] (which the Daylamites will fail to suppress) and inspiring the terrifying heresy of the Tajlideeya, These who will attempt the surgical transfiguration of entire populations whom they will then worship as newborn gods.[14]

Inquisitors arriving to audit irregularities in the worship of the Living God and Enoch his Prophet were told that the demiurge had taken Enoch to heaven, after successfully evangelizing to the rebellious angels in Hell. Aesculapius had fashioned the idol to fill Enoch's place in the mind of god, lest the subtraction of a righteous man from a depraved people tempt the

---

[11] Students wishing to contextualize this passage in the devolving Darwinia of hells should consult Bint Zaidiyya's *The Cultivation of Torment*.

Less reliable, the Ajami Private Diction, with its hideous mutation and emanation of data, has produced the following less atrocious examples:

The hell of immaculate still births, where the ululations of women are only made bearable by the laughter of half-made mouths and the absence of relieved spouses.

The hell of silent sirens, where the men who drown themselves only imagine they hear giggling.

The hell of the handless outcasts. Even the untouchables weep for them, for, the untouchables, at least, can touch themselves.

A contemporary sketch show imagines the damned as snowmen trembling beneath the smoke of three active volcanoes.

[12] Qattmir writes "become."

[13] The Persian historian Mirkhond accuses Aesculapius of forcing the followers of the living god to have sex with idols.

[14] The name of the sect means *bookbinders*. In esoteric terminology it also refers to the unbinding of human molecules to reveal an "inner text" superseding all the scriptures of the visible world. The rumors that the Tajlideeya bound their holy books in leftover human skin appear to be an orthodox fantasy or counter-revolutionary propaganda.

Maker's indecisive wrath in the instant between his eternally[15] destroying and remaking the world.

The iconoclasts bursting through to the rostral pedestal found no idol to smash. It was rumored that Aesculapius had hidden Enoch in a supernal minaret, quarantined from the sinful miasma of man.

Pilgrims arriving to worship Enoch found only Aesculapius scraping his flesh onto the altar, honing the 8-fold path— skinning, erosion, excision, incision, resection, contortion, constriction, lyes. If the pilgrim wished to stay, pray, performing the ra'ka in silence, they would soon witness a metamorphosis, 8,000 years before Ovid, dying in the penal colony of Tomis, breathes Victor Hugo's epitaph[16] through the Frenchman's unborn lungs. To each pilgrim, the god-king's pensive attendants gave a burin, a knife, a chisel and wax, acidic lyes, fat-eating mites and fungi, necrotic gels and a peeling tincture of realgar, wolf's milk and alkali of lime. Even The Omnipotent could not exalt the Highest One any higher. To honor Enoch, they must degrade themselves.

The crowds would slip about, dribbling pools of oils and viscera. The staff would half-molest, half-arouse the crowd. Temple convulsionaries danced airby, cutting themselves, sprinkling blood into the hair of zealous reverents stretching themselves across wire frames until they snapped their bones. Some succumbed to their holy wounds. Others gave up, only to be murdered by unaffiliated cultists on the road home. A few went mad from the pain and prophesied, pounding their chests as they

---

[15] The heresiarch Bar Dujayl, in a private recension of the Monomer of Enoch (edition of 80 episcripts, 167 W.E., Gurjan) insists on transcribing this word as "continuously," a substitution which will rally a quarter of the Sanhadjan world to the shalish of the infallible muraabit Bint Halima Mashadie, The Breaker, i.e. The Breaker of the Wheel of Suffering. Against Ibn Khaldun's theory of dynastic decline (vigor, decadence and only then the fall), the Mashadites will destroy the Daylamite-Hamajee dynasty at the height of its fanaticism and power.

[16] "Gentle, austere, my present refuge. My future tomb."

would the skulls of heretics and screeching holy writ in esoteric orangutan.

Inspired, a group of devotees colonized the open sahn. Shops sprang up, thriving towns, an empire with aqueducts to channel water from the 18 ablution fountains to the suburbs of the nascent oligarchs. Wars were fought for control of the nave, or a sacred arcade of the mihrab. Trenches spread like human veins around a quavering candle which attendants claimed could only be extinguished by the winter breath of primeval giants (man had shrunk since Adam's era). holy wars and mad assaults soon filled these trenches with their predestined blood.

Eighty-eight years passed.[17]

Aesculapius remained in embryon. He did not hatch.

In *The Debasement Books* we find the following:[18]

To debase himself...

We are told that Aesculapius carved idols from his own flesh to increase the number of Enoch's disciples, that he disfigured himself until he came to resemble the master. By those less credulous, that he wore an effigy of wood or a mask of pounded brass.

To debase the world...

Bar Ujayfi, who heard it from Bar Miqraad, says that Aesculapius built a panopticon of 888 concentric and orbiting spheres. Into each sphere, he poured seas and molten continents and colonized their cooling crusts with those he converted. In the central sphere he set the original Enoch of ivory, the All-colored, the Colorless. Over the second, two idols of flawless emerald. Over the third, three idols of gold. The fourth, of silver, and those next of marble, glass,

---

[17] An improbable chronology unless, following the apocryphal book of Genesis, we accept that the early patriarchs lived, on average, six or seven hundred years.

[18] Bar Ballaj proposes that the books are the surviving fragment of Enoch's "Effigies," a series of false biographies and molecular simulacra.

unseasoned cedar, paper, flax, mud, trash, until in the 888th sphere he made 888 Enochs out of feces. These, alone, Aesculapius felt worthy to worship. And these Enochs, in turn, did not despise their disciple.

To debase the world...

Aesculapius took entire cities hostage. He built new worlds and made new Enochs for his new worlds to worship. When anyone questioned his authority in these matters, Aesculapius, "like a wise man," had recourse to Enoch, whose silence was sufficient to answer any question.

When his cities were emptied and his armies exhausted, he had his sculptors sculpt the kafirs who lived beyond the Surrounding Sea, then fedayeen to purge them, atheists to jeer at both sides, heretics to betray them.

And when his craftsmen had finished these idols, he forced them to make idols of all his armies and a second copy of every idol made up to that moment and an idol of Aesculapius and all who had ever lived, in epic or prosody, and all of the dead. Last, he had them make idols of themselves and these he drowned in the Surrounding Sea along with their makers. And these idols, according to that most faithful witness Bint Hassiba Slimane, who told it to Bint Rabi'a in the year of her manumission, can still be seen swimming aside the ships of deep-sea sailors, as though waiting to be rescued. Many have tried, but the idols cry so pitifully that the sailors are compelled to free them from their nets.

To debase his disciple...

Enoch did as Aesculapius asked.

The promised metamorphosis is nowhere described at length. Bar Junayd, whose father was strangled for far less perverse speculation, prudently declines to record it. We have the partial abridgement in the Mukhtasar, an equally oblique allusion in the "Sirr Al-Asrar" and the gloss of Bar Junayd's inveterate enemy Bar Hallaj, who describes the metamorphosis as follows:

"And it was reported by the greenness of grass, the rage of the thunder, the bird as it soars over the crags of the Lips, the Teeth, of the Celestial Daaf, to fall exhausted or dead into its own reflection in the waters of the River Kerkur...that in that year the grapes did not ripen and the wine tasted like urine. And dunes as large as mountains absorbed the great monsoon so that there was not even dew to clothe the flowers, and then the people starved and parents traded children with their neighbors, so neither would grieve as much to pound strange urchins into mash. In that year, a change occurred. In the inner sanctum, before an inner circle of his beloved, Aesculapius poured molten brass over his entire body. And the finest brassworkers molded the features of Enoch over Aesculapius' screaming mouth, the delicate[19] work taking "exactly 16 days."[20]

An annihilation of self, prefiguring the <u>fanaa</u> of the Sufi mystics—to die before dying. In this way, at last, Aesculapius exalted Enoch by erasing himself.[21]

Appendix: A May-Or-May-Not Chronology

From Eve came Cain and after 300 years, Cain murdered Abel. And Eve and Lilith mourned him 100 years.

From Cain came Seth. From Seth came Kainan. From Kainan came Hagar. From Hagar came Cain. From Cain came Anosh, who ate the livers of his slaves and became his slaves, bite by bite. From Anosh came Enoch. Seven generations.

---

[19] Delicacy was essential, as the law declared it was death for anyone but his personal physician to touch the skin of the god-king.

[20] A measure which Mirkhond, who is everywhere gullible, considers too short.

[21] Latter-day da'is in the frontier jihad liked to practice what they called the gnosis and "self-annihilation" of Aesculapius, a process described in *The Fanaa of Hermes Trismegestius called Aesculapius,* a dialogue and manual of molecular suicide attributed to oral recordings taken by Aesculapius' immediate disciples. In actuality, a forgery as spurious as the "table talk" of the fictional reformer Martin Luther.

Apocrypha One: The Skull of the Mother

Bar Huthayl says. "Aesculapius did not build worlds. He rebuilt minds. Minds that could not believe in rival worlds."

"In those eddic days, Adam's gigantic wife had not yet putrefied. So Aesculapius, faithful to Adam's dying word, built a temple inside the corpse of Eve."

Bar Dujayl describes the dream he had on first reading the account of Bar Huthayl:

"And in my wine I saw the load-bearing ribs of Adam's wife. A garland of pixegrated eyes and coruscending hands, scoliotic minarets and domes rolling on pendentive tongues. And bowels where shadows burned with tormental fire, where species, blind since primal time, died of missing eyes. A blasphemy of bestial parts all praising god, their every cell dragging the divine down into our human muck."

In a later era, Piranesi[22] would reimagine this organic mosque in his *Perspectives, Antiquities, Grotesques*.[23]

Despite the fugue and fog of the source material, Piranesi's work depicts, with great precision, the stars, the remedies, the charms, devices, the wants, the repulsions of the people of a future and wholly organic world. The text, Piranesi left unfinished to suggest that this world was but the thinnest slice of a cosmos whose cubic mass was twice and twice again infinite.

Apocrypha Two: The Imposter

The account of false Adam, born 300 years after Lilith and Eve killed their treacherous husband. According to the *Fihrist*, that

---

[22] Engraver of fictional prisons.
[23] Leiden Edition. Twenty-six plates.

shifting ideogram of knowledge, the Imposter wrote the first alphabet on "the dust of his own body," i.e. baked clay, baked over the burning bodies of the pre-Adamite Adams.[24] The sons of Noah saved this tablet from the Flood, the seed of Ham dug it up, the wife of Zuhayr reintroduced poetry into the world.

Compare this to the isnaad of Juhani. "I was told by Urqud who heard it from Bint Mithana who...(here we abridge the chain of witnesses) that "the first Adam wrote on clay, the sixth preserved it, the tenth taught language to those who had not only lost their libraries but had forgotten how to <u>think</u> their own names."

---

[24] "As each eternity ends, their flesh regrows without aid of miracles."

DIPYGVS

The Eyes of Odysseus

In *The Odyssey*, Homer forgets to write that Polyphemus plucks the second moon and freezes it in Mount Etna's snow, the moon which is the entire world and every molecule, so that it too has its ships and fleeing Ithacans.[25] The cyclops inserts the moon into his empty socket and picks at it incessantly. Let it scab, let the itching drive him mad. He'll scratch until he sees nothing but Odysseus.[26]

Lip Reading

To relieve his subjects of their many burdens, Abu Mansoor Nizaari Al-Mustafa Ladeen il-Llah instructs his artisans to build a hive of living glass in the Mahdiya Mosque in place of the traditional pillbox (maqsurah) meant to shield the caliph against schismatics and assassins. The caliphal images, like chromosomes in odd mitosis, divide in proportion to the Muslim population (doubtful converts and People of the Book

---

[25] So that it too has its moons and raving Polyphemus...

[26] We find in Vasari's *The Lives of the Most Eminent Painters* a curious diametry, the apocryphal history of that stone Medusa which Leonardo painted on a wooden shield, as though no other reflection were possible.

excluded). Three times a day the commander of the faithful and his microbial images[27] intercede on behalf of every male Muslim,[28] freeing the believers to pursue the other Six Pillars— fasting, charity, purity, authority, the hajj, and the frontier jihad. A frugality which assumes that The All-Seeing One can read lips.

Karyotype

The aesthete Walter Pater—whose heart, according to Oscar Wilde, "beat twice for every pulse"—urged every artist to be "his religion's chief infidel."

"To burn always with that hard gemlike flame. This is success in life." To burn...to be heretic, inquisitor, ashes charring my cremation fire.

Bar Dujayl, who bowdlerized Pater to suit the dainty decadence of the skyminders of Akhua, says that it is equally repugnant to be the ovum or the clone. He petitioned the civil arrondissements to randomize their children, consistent with the ethics of germline engineering, or at least allow their natural sons to inherit one or two harmless dynastic errors.

---

[27] To prevent a dangerous multiplication of rivals, the qadis charge the more ambitious images with idolatry and blind them with acid. Specious charges, as reflections arranged in an unbroken circle could not help but pay homage to each other.

[28] The traditionists, relying on an unbreaking chain of transmission, confirm that the venereal prayers of male family members, real or holographic, are sufficient to inoculate their entire harem.

The Soldiers Mirror

Hafiz calls the cup of wine—Sikander's mirror.

After Alexander kills Cleitus[29] during a drunken feud, he groans "my cup is vinegar." A quadroon pun whose quarters are: the bitter repercussions of alcoholism, the rotting body of his best commander, the prudent tears which declaim "Par che amaro. Everything sweet has soured" to Cleitus' mutinous admirers, the morale of Alexander's troops spoiling beneath the suns of Sind and Afghanistan.

Alexander repeats that phrase—"my cup is vinegar"—years earlier, as he pours the funeral libations for the god-king Darius, anointing, defiling, forgetting that as vinegar is a prophecy of wine, so the rotting god-king reflects what Alexander's flesh will become. He has ignored the words of Thomas Browne, his ancestor in the cyclical time illuminated by "The Ornament of Stainless Light."[30] Browne, who might have chided that "more walk below the soil than upon it" and among these were more apparitional conquerors than all the regal images Alexander had ever bestowed on the mirrors of Persia, Greece or Babylon.

---

[29] Last of the old guard. Straight-shooter. Alexander preserves and promotes him as propitiation to his father's ghost. Murdered by way of premeditated rage for reminding his master's son that "with this hand, I saved you at the River Granicus." Alexander grieves and erects a shrine to his newly suspected divinity.

[30] The Soil of Rebirth nourishes a family tree in which a man may bud simultaneously as the leaves of a trillion entwining ancestral branches, to be his own grandfather, ape-father, the paraxial flagellum of the first vibrio cholerae bacterium, the single-celled Adamic molecule (or the twisted helices—Adam/Eve).

Of other mirrors, the Macedonians call their shield, a veneer of bronze over oak, the "Mirror of Perseus."[31] Aristobolus (or his interpreter) claims that the shields reflected their enemies' own terror back at them. Pioneering psych-ops or hostile lampoon?[32] Napoleon's dictum on bad morale as the oracle of defeat comes to mind.

In T.H. White's *The Once and Future King,* the teenage Lancelot is driven to become the greatest soldier in the world after seeing his own ugliness in a shield. "Food for powder" is how Anne Wesley ordains her runtish son Arthur Wellington, Napoleon's predestined conqueror.

Dr. McGrigor relates that the Iron Duke wept as the English "forlorn hope" (Craufurd's Light Brigade) assaults the Spanish fortress of Badajoz, the men behind impaling those in front on barricades of Toledo steel until, by the light of Congreve rocket-fire, the redcoats shone like coruscending mounds of butterflies.[33]

Appalled, Wellington orders the withdrawal. The body count is thousands known and unknowable.

Medals, euphemisms follow. An Indian monsoon of British phlegm.

Among the names which mistakenly appear on the regimental medal rolls is that of an orderly who had been cut in half by a cannonball nine years earlier at the Battle of Assaye, as Wellington's sepoy army tried to ford the Kailna River before the Marathas could reform their lines. Horrified witnesses attest that

---

[31] As "eagle wings in the egg presuppose air" (as Newton presupposes apples, stars) so the soldier, reflected in the shield, presupposes the shield. Thus the petcheneg clad in conniving god-skins are called "Sons of the Shield" which seems, at first, an antique metaphor.

[32] The posthumous resentment of besotted hagiographers and toy historians.

[33] McGrigor, a fervid if incompetent Arabist, adds, "I do not know whether he wept or whether I was wept."

the sagging horse and stump appeared to dance a minuet with their own reflections but, faithful to the strictures of that prudish dance,[34] avoided all lewd collisions with both their undine partner and the troops coming up from behind.

In 1812,[35] Wellington weeps over the fallen.

In 1803, Wellington weeps. His tears fall, forgotten, into the Kailna River. His army safe across, Wellington orders his commanders to extend the line in both directions, reasoning that the Maratha Army must follow suit or allow the British to turn their flanks. Squeezed between the Juah and Kailna rivers, the Marathas would not be able to deploy their superior numbers. But unexpectedly Wellington reverses himself, misled by bad advisers who report chaos in the Maratha lines. Wellington's center advances in good order, eager to take advantage.

In 1812, Wellington, swept by aberrant waves of passion, orders the immediate enfilade of Badajoz with two full divisions over the protests of his staff officers who fear that this "mass diversion" will blunt the main assault, or worse, compound the disaster by piling hundreds more onto the sacrificial altar. The 5th Division and Picton's 3rd cross the River Guadiana under a lawnmowing fire and do their best to draw some of the French furor away from the British center. Instead, they miraculously[36] seize the bastion of San Vicente, though the 3rd is decimated and Picton grievously wounded.[37]

In 1803, Wellington is defeated. Crushed, in fact, by the concealed reserves of the Raja of Berar, who had screened themselves behind the Maratha line. As news of the disaster

---

[34] The waltz had only just begun to scandalize the English grandees.

[35] The year in which Fourier receives the grand prize from the Institut de France for his prenatal superposition principle. We are made of time, hermaphrodites of different eras. As our molecules collide and grind, they leave behind a residue, the average reality of our daily experience.

[36] "A miracle to mortal view, but long tradition makes it pass for true."

[37] And Fitzroy Somerset, first to mount the breach, earns that glory and promotion which will allow him, as Lord Raglan, to lead that other Light Brigade to its doom.

reaches Britain, escutcheons stain in alarming numbers. Derided as a failed Sepoy General, Wellington sinks into obscurity,[38] one more inbred grandee of the despised Anglo-Irish ascendancy, a formidable viceroy's minor brother.

In 1812, the British flag flies over the citadel of Badajoz.

Vengeance follows. A massacre of 4,000 Spanish civilians. The French garrison suffers fewer losses.

To a man who asked, long after, "to what do you attribute your victories?" Wellington replied. "All that is India."

"And India?" asked the man.

"Badajoz."

⊕

Bovinterlude

It describes as follows. The milk comes first, the cows come after if so desired. The cow "becomes," in the language of the Neoplatonists, and vanishes, but not before we squeeze a dozen thin but refreshing liters from its dissipating udders.

⊕

Doublekind

From the Grecian *Cornucopia of Abelard*:

"At the predestined moment, the kings threw their spears. The one struck Alexander, or his driver, in the head. The other pierced the throat of the Persian driver and hurled him left, his spasmodic hands still clutched the reins, the horses panicked, the chariot flipped. At that moment, Alexander's chariot rammed into his, throwing Alexander across erupting wood, horse and bronze.

"Now Perdiccas, alerted to the disaster, immediately led a detachment of the somatophylake to save their king. Seeing the wreckage sinking beneath a foaming sea of horses, the imperial

---

[38] Sir John Moore, who does not die at Corunna, goes on to fight Napoleon at Waterloo.

bodyguards had already begun to mourn the death of their hopes (and to scheme for the coming power struggle), when the two kings emerged, unharmed.

"For a moment they stood, challenging or cursing each other. But as the first was struggling, by common agreement, to put on his helmet in order to continue the duel, the other treacherously began fleeing towards the Persian lines. Some of the somatophylakes, recognizing the ram horns of Alexander, carried the fainting conqueror to safety. The rest pursued Darius, but a Persian counter-charge scattered them.

Quintus Curtius tells us that Perdiccas, with a manful submission to fate, examined the bodies with a conscientiousness that belied his disappointment. The chariot wheel had split the driver's head like a winter melon. Now Perdiccas was a man with no head for faces. We are told that he reintroduced himself to his own betrothed on three separate occasions, twice during the ritual gift exchange. There appears to be some corroboration for this. A fragment of Nearchus has Perdiccas introducing himself to a mirror. Thus he poured the funeral libations but could not say the words. For he, a devotee of Demeter and privy to the undercore of the Eleusinian Mysteries, could not in good conscience commend a stranger to that unseen queen."

The gloss of Abelard, his naïve decryption:

"...this unnamed witness claims to have been present in the secret sanctum to witness Alexander's birth, the excision of the parasitic twin,[39] the body-double which cleaves, by god-affliction, to the pelvic bone of the kings of Earth, harvested upon gestation and grown in grinding obscurity. Awaiting the Day of Emergence when both will rule the world until one, by common conspiracy, falsely slays the other."

---

[39] What the semantic otakus, the jingoes for lingo, call a cryptodidymus.

THE DIVINE ROXANNE

A Robin Red breast in a Cage
Puts all Heaven in a Rage
—William Blake

⊕

In one way, Alexander the Great's bride is less than immaculate.
They have kept her quarantined since she was a girl. Like the
gerygone bird,[40] trained to adorn the chambers of provincial
satraps in utter silence, she has never learned to sing, or even sign,
the songs of her sistern.

Her voice, when it erupts, will drive her husband mad. Her
operatic daughters will burst, in vitro, from her lovers' throats.

⊕

Others—subsets of ourselves—say she was bred, a larval
androgyn leaning femme. Bred to practice higher crafts together
with the Kama Sutra: enigmas, mines and quarries, disputation,
the cultivation of flower carriages, erotic anagrams, cabals. Ready
to engage the princes—leaning male—at their discretion, whose
days are devoted to snail fighting and pelting each other with
Kadamba flowers and the supple delectation of <u>kartari</u>, both a

---

[40] The gonadal gerygone bird—born of sound and birthing it.

kind of erotic dance and the cutlass edged in acid used to scar the dancer and her client, a postwar map of border scars, drawn to placate puppet princes, ensuring future civil wars.

And he the prince? The current breeding bitch of our Visceral Queen, she of the Sphere of the Core of the Worlds, whose empire compared to Alexander the Great's domain is as radar screen to false radar blip?[41]

The prince is gluing tiny wings to his stumps, so deftly sutured and benign of scars that even the embryonic mirrors of the Pleasure Palace, having once adored a seraphim, reject this slithering slug as an imposter, refusing him their reflections.[42]

He is a body without wings. He is seraphim, of the Little Aileron, cloud saints, a cloud race but lovely, a worthy hostage diadem to crown a conqueror, the body tribute his celestial country pays for peace, whose soldered stumps the poet Bar Dujayl once eulogized and compared to the amputated towers of Tinjitan. Tinjitan, whose mornings are mourning furnaces, whose stars are the senile eyes of god.

---

[41] That tragic or foreordained false flag which detonated the civil war between our Inside and their Outside world, between their Inside and their Outside worlds, etc., 888 cascading civil wars.

[42] For the odd mitosis of these nomadic emanations and the anachronistic organisms (museums of past and future molecules) which gestate from eidolon overlapping eidolon, see Qitmir's note in *The Astral Chronography of Shahs*, episcript (ES) GC_A5683 in the Hezerdja Patrimonial Archives, or the more easily obtainable epitome of Bar Junayd.

Harpalus,[43] in a lost letter to Aristotle, is the first to observe that
the breeding ant, the alate male, sprouts wings only once, for the
nuptial flight. Afterwards, the pregnant hymenettes bite the wings
off their discarded lovers and spray the males with a digestive
enzyme before setting them to build precursor mounds to house
the budding brood of working femmes. The males often work
themselves to death long before they are devoured.[44]

For eight years, the prince has secretly curated these alate
males, of that titanic species *gargantua deformis conjugens,* until in
the breeding season there were hundreds of precursor mounds
and millions of colonists swarming from his sham apartment on
25 Rue Hibel in the tariqa of La Mameet Jambe, a bubbling burb
in the antique city-room Odah, a room set aside for his adult
amours[45] whenever the queen was busy "mounting the stalls" of
other breeding sons,[46] the scions of allied dynastic nahis, client
mawlas, the hostage wards of defeated Hamajee tribes, a room
the size of a city in a hallway the length of the world, the only
city-room in the seraglio of the queen's Pleasure Palace where
the streets were blind, stripped of spying ganglions, where the
people were people and not maphrians, subdermal informants

---

[43] The huckster and mercenary myrmecologist who supplies Alexander
with a regular subscription of the Greek tragedians—Aeschylus, Sophocles,
Euripides, other proper nouns now lost to us. A foxtail embezzler. Renault
speculates that Aristotle's at times absurd zoology owes something to this
practical jokester. The philosopher had commissioned Harpalus to report
back on Eastern fauna. Executed after a hustle gone sour.

[44] Bint Utbah suggests that this ruthlessness—the "castrated" males are
utterly docile—stems from a vestigial fear of an extinct subtype of terrorist
male.

[45] Dalliance as pressure valve. By law, the prince's sexual needs were
deemed "insatiable."

[46] A sexual tour of duty requiring seven months.

infesting deluded corpses. Odah, with 16 million configurable citizens,[47] banks, florists, herbariums, warehouse pornography, a quantum bandes dessinées comic where each panel gestates nine child panels (nine choices or destinies) then dies like any other organism, no-minder immigrants from barbaric city-rooms two doors down, parents with mouths to feed, their children— paycheck moths, schooligans pricking delirium™, petit plebians, cult babies, diapered pensioners, manufactured moons, moons for every mood, a love cafeteria where lovers eat each other, become each other and themselves, the crater of Bint Marjane Sanjil where Saksiwa and his shuhada' suckle sacs of methane gas and feed themselves to the Maternal Fire, ascetics circumcised up to the neck, a Mob (or Mass) armed with industrial flamethrowers, for they the citizens of Arrondissement Mettijet have discovered that a fireman, a local hero, is a child molester so they are burning down all the houses he has saved these past 20 years, reasoning— with perfect justice—that the works of evil men must be evil, altruistic vampires with a thirst for giving blood, conspiracy radios, a body-politic as body-horror film, two nasik subedars about to assassinate each other, having mistaken the other for the reclusive messiah of the ruling cabal, a terrorist sect called "Codon" composed entirely of police informants, stomach factories, senators colonizing other senators, a tapas restaurant called "Foreplay," a literary magazine entitled *Monomer,* welders, the stars in middle age or the dimmering eidola of stars, pub trivia, jazz clubs, threnos (communal grieving), communal guillotines, tennis courts, slums, algorithmically generated historians, a library whose most popular volumes are a series of fission fables by the celebrated pediatrician turned children's author Bint Mithana, complete with pop-up mushroom clouds which emit harmless

---

[47] With personas to whet his whims and a rotating tasting menu of ethnic tensions, manifest destiny, high-minder nihilism, civic hysteria. On average, the ottamati of the civil arrondissements import about 82,088 no-minder strangers to replenish the citizens who die in *le grande dérange,* the upheavals, scheduled schizophrenia and cosmetic surgery of crowds necessary to appease the harem's inexhaustible appetite for novelty.

but detectable levels of radiation, refinery explosions, a button to plunge mankind into a twilight so charming that dalliance and (sanctioned) adultery are all but assured.

⊕

He sits and reminisces about the future. With foresight, he hopes to deter the past. He ages now, this young immortal, older than his eventual corpse. Time has cracked its chasms before, behind him. He has no wings to fly across the gaps.

⊕

Hell is a cellar, a sewer, a subway station. Tonight (which night? which escape attempt?) he sleeps in Hell, stuffed into one of the coffin blocks which make up the subway ceiling. He is sleeping, but his wings continue to soar on wisps of Paradise thinner than the alpine ghosts of the Celestial Daaf. Ready to flee pursuing sounds.

⊕

His wings are screaming. Rough surgery. Masks and nitrile gloves. They have sedated his body, but his wings continue to kill, enveloping the face of the assistant surgeon and twisting, tossing head and C1 and C2 vertebrae into the operating theater stalls, scattering students and spraying blood in absurdist paintings across the surgeons' scrubs. They're forced to strap him down. The wings heal as quickly as the electric teeth can chaw, forcing the surgeons to chop The wings slip from their bonds, thrust upwards, towing some braying hostage by one leg towards the skylight set in a cupola which seems always on the brink of caving in. It takes five substitute saints[48] to pin them down with nails as thick as oil pipes. The disposal units are overanxious. They set

---

[48] The fanatic altruists of the PSC (Private Service Communes).

the theater on fire. The medical staff is forced to evacuate, in their panic they almost abandon the prince on the melting operating slab.

⊕

In the death of every ant he found a kind of change. What changed? He didn't know. Every change was a kind of death, so why agonize over that final death? Unless death was not the final step and decay was life, a ripening into the past. Thus the maggot, writhing corpses eating corpses, who coruscend to life as flies.

⊕

His fingers are meant for delicate work, those of an effigist, polymerist, anatomist, pianist. The most difficult part is plucking the wings without killing the males, or rupturing the membrane so like the lava plains of the antique hajj. His prayer is always the same. He begs his flesh as he implants each wing, to compel each tiny pinion to resume their proper shape, to <u>be</u> celestial cells, coverts, feathers, scapular. He begs and whips himself raw.

⊕

In this way he sprouts useless wings. Why wings, if vestigial? Wings were for queens, not for slaves. Why not when he has nothing to do between regal visitations but to waft erotically (actually he <u>walks</u>, but even the word "walk" repulses him) like the smoke of brandy-butter cigarettes across cocktail parties, the kind where men disguise themselves as themselves, where women swap lips and structural ribs, where origami odalisques fold into gravitational geometries, deranging their clients and themselves.

⊕

He is addicted to astral air, the moonrays drilling through his scalp, the hallucinogenic herd of nephilim which form the southern aurora, the clouds, like dragon-lamenting flames, the pedesis, or manic fluctuation of cherubim bouncing skull on skull, a shower of star chunks hard enough to crunch his fish-fragile bones, the riddle of a lightning bolt which no man (or jinn) can answer, the answer of the thunder cloud.

⊕

There is a date on the calendar which he ignores. The only rigorous refutation of solipsism that he knows, more rigorous than his tutors' overpriced sophistries, is that however much he ignores, neither the calendar nor the queen nor her entourage disappear. And the queen remains punctual.

Tired of painstaking work under a microscope, he smothers his stumps. Gluing the wings to his legs, his shoulder blades, his waist, his lips, under a mesh of mollificant powder to dehydrate and seal. Blending his body until his body disappears.

⊕

"It did that," the queen would say, dreamily denying complicity, believing *de tres bon Foi* that all actions were history and history was destiny and right away the royal carpets would ripple (too timid to tremble) from 300,000 petticoat ministers drumming their approving faces against the floor. The dominant school of historical astrology often took a generous view of her inevitable atrocities. While the scientists of the aqala al-shuhaada denied the existence of atrocity <u>and</u> history, as neither could be reproduced in the lab.

⊕

The city-room is shutting down for emergency maintenance. Blackout in five...four...the prince has barely enough time to throw

on a burda to conceal the royal prerogative, i.e. his nakedness, and
to hide his new wings before fleeing Odah.

It's a moonless night, but he sees by reflected darkness as
men by light. He feels like diving as he used to dive into the abyss
of the sky, which is madness for the walls of the Pleasure Palace
are made of eyes. He leaps from stairs, from zeppelin shelves,
knocking over and shattering a gourd, the last surviving relic,
or replica, of the defeated tribes of the Hamajee Veldt. He fills
an empty swimming pool, drained two months past after the
tainted chlorine blinded two of the queen's favorite "stallions," with
pristine mattresses stolen from Depot Q5 West.

He sneaks into the ballroom and tames the bestial arabesques
and meaty bas relief of the walls whose contraversal faces both
whine and cheer, sneer or mother him with baby blandishments.
Even the more sympathetic of them try to buck him off like a
flea, but he clings and clambers over tigers, theluuls with vestigial
eyes, a quartet of owls hooting smutty madrigals, vaporous garai,
swinging himself up by the ear of the devious panther who first
set the "carnivore" and the "herbivore" at war with each other. He
leaps...tries to leap, slips and falls. Never has he fallen. To fall is
impossible. The contraversal faces set aside their differences. They
laugh at him in bipartisan glee.

⊕

Once, after the queen had left him *le petit morts*, he had this bitter
thought. We touch but do not touch, fuck but do not fuck. So the
pandars of electromagnetism attest, that the more our particles
attract, the more they repel until our loathing could repel the god
of love itself.

⊕

A seraphim's legs are like broken crutches.

For the first two months after the amputation he could only crawl. His skin putrefies from dovish to cirrhotic yellow. He mourns the Sky as a widower mourns his wife.

In the third month he learns to walk. His body weighs too much. With every step he seems to sink deeper beneath the sod.

Exhausted, he dreams of Lucifer crashing into bolts of lightning until they shatter even that adamantine body. In this way that arch rebel surpasses god. The immortal kills himself and nullifies omnipotent power.

$$\oplus$$

He knows he will never fly again.

The crying baca-androgyne of his empress have purged the mounds with blasting nozzles, cut the low-minder drones apart with jets of boric acid, swept away the fighting femmes, the pregnant hymenettes, the hymenuptial tsarinas who dommed with twats of steel, the no-minder hostages from rival mounds. Millions of ants in whorls of crumpled thoraxes, ruptured abdomens, sheared antennae and faces diced to gory trellises. Millions of alate breeding males streaming from the broken windows of his sham apartment.

The androgynes are tearing out his wings as tenderly as a Hamajee heart wife might pluck her husband's beard on the eve of war to preserve a follicle for the Day of Resurrection.

$$\oplus$$

It is autumn and from Alaganda Park, leaves are wafting through the windows of his sham apartment, ant wings wafting by the clump, dead things swirl on supernal winds. He has submitted so tamely that when he goes limp they drop him in surprise and before one seraphic knee has graced the ground, he bounds and corkscrews through the broken window.

Two androgynes dive for his legs, slamming and impaling him on jagged glass. For a moment he teeters on the sill. The extra weight from his remaining wings is just enough to tip them screaming off the ledge.

Here the odd mitosis of the tale divides. In one version, an absentminded god transmutes his supernal son into a cloud (or compassionately deranges his mind so that he believes in his own cloudiness). In the other, the prince rejects the fraud and falls.

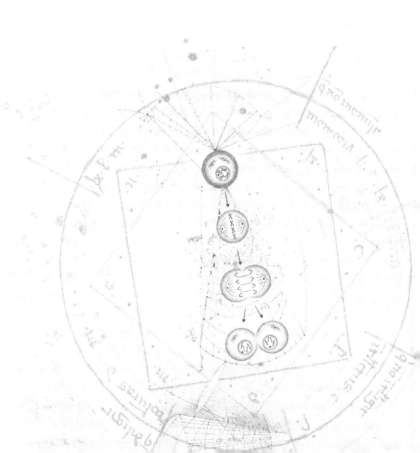

THE PATCHWORK COMPENDIVM

Dedicatory Remarks

I build a monolith of my sister's arms, her hips, her teeth, her ears.
An anthology of body parts, a patchwork compendium.

As you climb, you will find that I have incised a may-or-
maybe memory into each part and molded each from scale model
casts of my sister's body, smuggled from the morgue with her
consent. I make no excuses. I do not evade arrest. This monolith is
my advocate.

⊕

Invocation

"We know the flesh only through his bones, the bones he cloaks
in putrid clothes," intones Bar Shibli of the man they flayed
against the Weirding Creed of God, his skinless master-martyr
Hallaj. According to the chain of transmission which begins with
Karnaba'i, Shibli stole what remained of Hallaj from the queen-
mother's museum of schismatic heads and entrusted it to the
Remnant hiding in Khorasan, and it is said the head will never
rot. As for Shibli "he made a prayer mat from his master's flesh."

⊕

Patchwork #0: Muqaddimah

I wonder, comcestral niece or great-granddaughter who read this inscription, if you know the word <u>maquette</u>, a word in the ancient patois-melange cognate with the Italian <u>bozzetto</u> of our Recombinant Mothers, a preparatory model for a sculpture or, in other contexts, the twisted helices, a tremulous sketch of blood. It would do reverence to your Blood to look up these words before climbing on. Remember, one day your bodies too may loom here with the rest of us.

⊕

Patchwork #GNRH1: The Scale Model

On her deathbed, #252 of 500 crowdfunded hospital tombs, I heard my sister paraphrase Proust. "The sculptor is tidying up." And then, perplexed. "The sculptor forgot the tits."

⊕

Patchwork #Msx2: Our Ladyneck of Worms

She is a budding taxidermist and she has found a headless bird with a maggot-neck of worms. A maggot is a breeding tomb, these cadavers give birth to flies.

Death does not bother her. What bothers her is that these maggots have vandalized the bird's final art, which the bird had sacrificed its life to sculpt.

Yi-Shuen grinds her teeth, flips the bird with a spatula into a ragged shoe, flicks the maggots into a pot of boiling coffee, skins and sprinkles borax on the feathers. She saves and stuffs 18 birds that summer, one rose-finch, three starlings and other names which I would only recall years later when I took up birdwatching in locales beyond the reach of cellphone towers to forestall a second intimation of divorce.

Patchwork #20E: Indulgences

"Death bothers me," she confesses to the stars.

She hunches her shoulders inwards as though she had butterfly wings vast enough to engulf herself and engender a kinder metamorphosis.

Patchwork #TBX4: Shahada

The 55th rak'ah and worming circumambulation rubs her belly raw.

"Com-passio-nate thy supplicant, Holy Worm which grows inside the Worm, Hole which grows inside the Hole." She worships. No one will think to connect this invocation and apostasy with her idolatrous body-mods.

Patchwork #18.01528: The Book of Water

"Man is but a book of water," according to the antique *Phrase Book of Innocuous Body Language*. Correct, but hyperbolic according to the latest science.

Of other people we only know their drier parts. And since we have found no Rosetta stone for "reading" human H_2O, I should forgive myself for how little I knew about my sister.

Patchwork #C5orf50: The Headless Head

For Halloween my sister dresses up as a headless David Hume. It's the year before she abandons me and switches majors from philosophy to biology (having dropped taxidermy, at age 16, as a "bit too goth"). Like all biologists she will be a tragic failure, unable to put the fundamental axiom of her own death to the test.

The costume is a tight fit.

"Please don't goose-step on our cat," I admonish as Yi-Shuen stumbles blindly. Our cat is less cat and more basic parlor tiger who does her best to simulate a big game hunter rug.

I see a girlike indentation through the neoprene neck. The indentation scowls. I think maybe she is not quite getting the effect she sought.

David Hume, let us not forget, was a philosopher of the World Before who denied the "I" (playfully, his enemies accuse) and advocated what Bint Mithana calls "bundle theory" which reduces the human mind to a plantlike array of sensors lacking any sense of self. Conspiratorially, Hume has been opposed by those I like to call dharmic materialists who think that you and I are only the residual slime of the real world as it slugs on by, with solipsists as a nervous buffer state between these two philosophic powers.

⊕

Patchwork #31: Beat Off

The Akhuan Institute has just denied her first research grant, but she twerks her neck sedately to some chillhop music. Characteristically her tantrum is days late in arriving. She always seems to act/react in the past, making cutting ripostes only after all the other banterers have moved on to other jokes, staring color-blind (she was never color blind) at traffic lights before finally hitting the gas, swatting xenophobically at flies who had long since emigrated to foreign noses. And if this makes sense: ducking a basketball that has already hit her in the nose.

⊕

Patchwork #Hs 738: The Host as Appetizer

I see a drooling mouth attached to a starving woman.

When her cancer spread from missing breasts to throat, even her own saliva burned like a lava flow. But her salivary glands continued to secrete with undiminished hope.

At last she decided to stop swallowing and let her mouth overflow and river down her chin and chest and make a marsh between her toes. Hunger did its digestive work.

I had just returned from the store with more painkillers or placebos. When I saw her, I was encouraged. She seemed the fattest I had seen her in many months.

Patchwork #p63: Mao for Precocious Grades 3 ̠ 12

I see the spongy lips of Mao Zedong chirping aphorisms, as his crony Chou En-Lai twitters madrigals in praise of ditch diggers filling mass bougie graves.

I point these resemblances out to my sister who raises her fist in response.

Of course she is the opposite of a mass murderer. She has a surgeon's hands, not pampered knockoff peasant hands, spilling red ink on death warrants, pruning the nation as a gardener, with juicy gloves, snips undesired stems from a tomato plant.

She's scheduled another struggle session, as I lounge in the other bed, knees crossed in faux sit-up stance, recounting fangirl filtered synopses of YA novels she does not allow herself to buy, omitting all plot details in favor of shipping character X and Y with the algebraic zeal of an al-Khwarizmi plagiarizing Hindu numerals. Meanwhile, Yi-Shuen breaks from protozoa to study chromatids, from chromatids to poring (sweaty hands, nerve problems) over cartoony coils of mRNA, stopping only to transcompose her self-made lesson plans into mimetic songs which she will gargle dusk to dawn in counterpoise to scenes of pixelated refugiados trudging down a trail of terrazzo tears blazing from our grandparent's fritzy qamariyya storyglass window.

⊕

Patchwork #46: Excerpt from the Phrase Book of Innocuous Body Language

"Crestrisen eyebrows indicate boredom waterlogged by a lusty flood." It was somehow appropriate that they never hooked up. She'd rather he drown, and self-reject, then have what she could never want.

⊕

Patchwork #88: The Finishing Touch

I cannot kiss her forehead because in a moment this forehead will no longer belong to her.

She is the shapeshifting sculptor of cursed power, with godlike control over every cell until 1 + that final moment dividing down to neverness. In neverness she cannot even touch herself.

⊕

Patchwork #17: Chicken in D Minor

When I asked her what she was listening to she replied, sticking her ragtag elbows out and pecking at the ground. "Bach, Bach," her favorite composer. "He's named after a chicken's cluck." Snooty chickens, I guess, but at six years old I took her at her bock-bock word.

⊕

Patchwork #NaN: The Gaybee Factory

The sign hanging across her chest reads "Open for Business."
Today she is a "gaybee factory" with fists on what she calls her
"queer-bearing" hips, inversion of her bully's "child-queering" taunt.

⊕

Patchwork #26: The Talkative Butter Knife

She is reading a butter knife, with which a little while ago she
feigned to "cut away" her missing breasts. I think it's a junk design
for decorating genuine silverware, but she runs her fingers over
it with all the ecstasy of an archaeologist decrypting crusted
hieroglyphics for the blind.

⊕

Patchwork #A-43818: The Twisted Helices

After the mastectomy, she lapsed into a morphine dream for
several hours. At around the fourth canon-hour, she awoke. I
cradled her as she cried. "I'm a biologist, nature's goddamn gift to
life, but I can't even prove I'm going to die..."

It was of the utmost significance, as deep an omen as any
bloodied wolf cub to our Conscript Fathers, that she came across
that Proustian line shortly after. The line reiterated her only
failing as a brilliant young biologist. She could not, being dead,
<u>falsify</u> her own death and thus her courage failed, and thus her
faith in science died.

⊕

Patchwork #A-43818: Addendum

We need not <u>verify</u> death. As Edward Young remarks. "All men
believe all men mortal but themselves."

Patchwork #PITX1: Buckshot Elegy

We park by the side of the road to infiltrate a PSC wheat field and record some parasite blog footage with the microcam, but most of it is pretty boring, except the aphids zeroing their cornicles, anti-predator wax launchers which fail to fend off the Nom Nom ladybugs.

Yi-Shuen is hobbling, but only when I go to dump the bathing basin do I see the blood. She admits, under interrogation, that private service commune farmer Shang's buckshot had "just" grazed her ankle, digging a canal straight through our family mark, a double flap of batwing flab, a wound which darkens in putschy shades of learlike purple for several months.

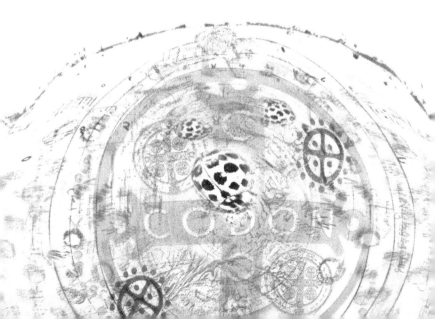

THE BVSTAAN OF BRVNCHLESS BARRY

The last of my brunch eggs died this morning.

I think this is how it happened, though by the time you finish reading this text you probably could have absorbed more wiki data about the osprey hawk and ornithology, the gagging regurgitation of which data will amount, in lieu of dad jokes— although I don't know if I see you as the <u>funny</u> dad, you know? More dadcore, dependable and...whew! Excuse me, I hope cell phone towers don't pick up fart jokes—Anypoo...will amount to a searing Summa Apologia in defense of the rudeness of toyminder texting culture and the obliviousness of your daughter's derelict college friends she claims she brought back with her because "we're total BFFs" and "facetime is just sooooo <u>impersonal</u>," even though you're sure that her friends are really here to act as a buffer between her and her parents, and yeah they're not listening to you and their noses are crinkling as you fart out trivium after trivium and shit, they've been awkwardly scrolling through that same text message for a long time now and so you go back to sipping your empty "GOAT Dad" coffee mug wondering what the fuck is going on when they suddenly decide to "Tik-Tok" for the amusement of Politburo hackers until you flee to your room where you'll stare into the mirror and suck in your flab and drop to the floor and do some crunches before giving up and rubbing one out while your second (third?) wife's jogging, not all the way out, maybe just enough to feel relevant again, all the while ignoring the fact

that those pornstars you're jerking to are probably not much older
than...well whatever, you'd probably learn more from wikipedia
than whatever this foodie eulogy could ever teach you. Really, it's
kinda worrying how much time you've wasted even reading this
far. This very sentence, this one here (the recent downturn is no
excuse for missing your vision insurance premium, especially if
you're going to leave those crusty contacts in for weeks at a time),
yep, this very word, or this one, could be the linguistic landmine
that sets off your inevitable data analytical aneurysm which would
at least mollify your boredom and your imposter syndrome and
the parasitical lie of a life well-provided infesting the minds of
your family—not that your second wife was ever worried seeing as
how her personal glass ceiling was a skylight up in the penthouse,
cause you know she actually got her masters, and a beaucoup
prenup, while your ceiling was more of a foggy ventilation window
somewhere down in the basement agri-data center. Gosh, I miss
those guys, don't you? I'm doing alright though. How weird is
it we got the exact same severance package?—sorry...infesting
the minds of your family who will find it too humiliating to
explain, even to the coroner, what you, a decorated wartime kevlar
crotch plate inspector, were doing when you died (later, forensic
investigators will accuse your son of opening several extreme,
though legal, subdermal genres of porn and a paramilitary
free-state fantasy message board in your internet browser in
an attempt to divert attention from the banality of your final
moments). But then what am I saying? There are billions of
human beings on the planet, and what are the chances that out
of the 67,000 people worldwide currently clutching their chests
like Kano from the original Mortal Kombat (some twerp the
other day asked me what an "SNES" was, *blow-my-brains-out
emoji*) that you of all no-minders should be among the 37%
actually dying of a heart attack or sorry, an aneurysm, and not
experiencing heartburn or phantom chestburster syndrome, and
in any case if you aren't dying then really this is a wake-up call
that you're kinda fucking over your real children by not preparing

a legally enforceable will that will protect them from Sharon's fucking udder-rutters or scratch that, <u>youthful indiscretions</u> which she, more power to her, decided to keep, but on the other hand if you <u>are</u> dying at least the resulting legal shenanigans might hide in plain sight exactly how small an inheritance you had to divy up in the first place but life's full of disastrous decision points isn't it? Anyhoo, it seems that the pesticide canisters donated by our local eco-PSC cellholders have been thinning out the shells of osprey eggs all summer, not that we don't appreciate the assist from our selfless private service communes. When the osprey-mom goes to sit on her eggs...smoosh! Or crunch, or I don't know what sound effect goes here, that's just how the infographic cartoon depicts it, and who am I to question the scientific credentials of livestreamer DewBagOcelot8998? Now I don't like to be fatalistic, but I have to read...give me a second...I have to finish reading this news feed which tells me that that within a day of exposure to "Brennan's D-720 MiteSmotherer" the egg shells had grown so thin that even if someone had had the foresight early on to gather the eggs into an electric incubator—baby osprey breast for dinner? Don't knock it—the eggs still would have burst like scrumptious face huggers.

Anyways, I just wanted to check in. Sorry to be all "mentoring my mentor on you." I just worry, you know? Staring at our little poop-machine's ridiculous baby chub right now and scrolling through want-ads and googling "how to dad," cause I mean with credit cards and car loans and student loans and cat toys anyone would freak out, especially at your age, but no, no, all totally understandable, we've all been there...I'm still there, Stuuuudeent Loaaanss...sigh. Guess that's what canned margarita is for. I'm so glad to hear that you're consolidating all that shit.

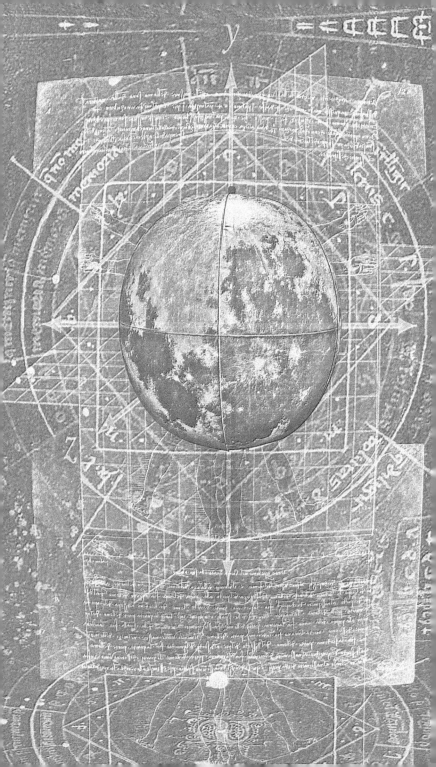

SELVES OF THEMSELVES

It is averred in *The Butter of Wisdom*, and other curious volumes
of Bar Hebraeus, that a wind which rustles samour leaves
is poisonous unless <u>purified</u>—<u>annihilated</u>, according to the
hostile translation of Bar Huthayl—by contrary air from the
Surrounding Sea.

    Whereas we find that from the pollution of otherwise
indistinguishable bodies proceeds our purest notions of space and
time.

    For if all bodies are one, motion is impossible. A body cannot
move away from itself. If we are one flesh, as the orthodox insist
we are, she cannot leave, but staying is illusional. All numbers are
identical. Counting and time are unthinkable. The door never
slams. She is always opening it. The left side of the pillow is
uncold and unwarm.

    Easier still, if no more rigorous. If all bodies are one, this
monomer is superfluous. Letters, however mutated, however
numerous, would all spell the same man.[49] Our arguments, and
their arguers, may be safely ignored.

---

[49] And that man would be monomer, polymerist, audience, destiny, a
slanderous biography of that destiny, the acronym DNA.

THE STARS IN MIDDLE AGE

The Spy or The Niche of Light

Father-mother of headless searchlight pedestrians, enjoyment brigades, *da'i* Sunshine Battalions ("insomnia fanatics" according to the hostile translation of Bar Huthayl), phosphorescent (nightglow) pedophiles.

Procurator of mandatory sunshine hours, emergency daylight powers, civic coffee roasters, ambient creeper beacons, all-seeing eye drops.

Regulator of bellytelly voyeurism, cornea curation credits.

His Mollitude in Middle Age means "lights-on" policies, eyelid-clefting initiatives, paid blackout benefits.

His void portends deepfake journalists, patriotic camera filters, gossamer skin transplants, transparency duty, pigment rations, plexiglass ovaries.

Illustrious Supplicants:

Ghrazali—"Sight is but one of the spies of intelligence,"

Kalman Tihanyi,

Otto Röhm,

Elmer Ambrose Sperry.

⊕

The Twins (Munis the Eunuch and Munis the Stud)

Regulator of solitary grief and threnos, communal grieving, moody moor ghosts, comedy vendettas, synchronous backstabbing, bitter number twos.

Father-mother of mole-men killed in grain-dust explosions, grudge grinders.

Rules the germination of dule, the "hanging tree" which is known to rot and shed its branches in repudiation of an unjust hanging.

Illustrious Supplicants:
Heathcliff,
The Union Leader Bint Zarush,
Metrodorus—"that the eyes of frightened and astonished people emit the stars which we call The Twins,"
La Vauguyon—who had the courage to shoot himself in the throat a second time.

Accidental Supplicants:
Origen.

$\oplus$

The Moon or The Blind Emissary

A kind of Sancho Panza whose gravitational influence keeps the Earth from wobbling or tilting disastrously and so smothering the temperate continents with ice.

Father-mother of emissaries, go-betweens, moderators, sacrificial oxen, borderless bodies, bridge molecules, lungs, herd whisperers, political moderates.

Nurturer of etymological ligaments, cock pic blockers, candied class motility stimulants, regulatory codons, palate cleansers.

Rules over fractions, conversational science, repartee, intoxication, syllables, soliloquy parsers, haakiya-mimics.

Her Mollitude in Middle Age means wartime ambassadors, nattering nudniks, frugal frenemies, headless mobs, headless anarchs and demagogues.

Her void portends disease ambassadors, gonzo participation parties, invertebrate sugar babies, ormach theater, whose pathos is not due, as the critics accuse, to the lucid musculature of the headless actors or their tremulous <u>body</u> language, but to the pity the audience feels knowing that the ormachs born and grown just before the opening curtain will be recycled right after the curtain drop (dropping like a redundant guillotine).

On Disease Ambassadors:

These include patient zeroes, bubonic fleas, wrath-borne disease (Cf. Yves de Kruif's *Parasites Célestes*, with 46 copper plate engravings of infested angel wings).

On Participation Parties:

"One remembers few <u>ceremonial</u> details or the finalists, so-called, but only the shaggy dog story told by Bar Shibli to the "Ornamatti"—rude misspelling of *Ornati*—Elder Bar Dubayr of the 59th Civil Arrondissement (Imperial Akhua) about Outremer outworlders who crash-land in an apocalyptic alien skyscraper and are eaten, after savage cubicle-to-cubicle combat, by feral office cannibals. Shibli's smartass petition for inclusion in the Hezerdja Patrimonial Anecdotal Archive was unanimously rejected by the Board, 7–0."

On Bodily Spasms:

In *The Augur's Book of Bodily Spasms*, the traveler "born above the moon" and suffering from the rare combination of gout, autonomic neuropathy, and regurgitation syndrome (small intestine dysmotility also rarely augurs well) is predoomed to arrive at the central island of a certain, fertile, archipelago, no matter which direction he travels.

On that island, long before he sees through fog that thing whose very shape is evil, the traveler will <u>smell</u> a rancid mountain, an intestinal mass, a fecal slaw of pupal kings, blindly gnashing, wriggling, strangling, sluddering single file up and through drooling sphincter valves, each to serve their turn at ruling the world.

Far below the valves—as far as the hawk who soars above the Celestial Daaf is from its eidolon soaring beneath the Sea of Qaf—is a sucking hole, a converse rectum slurping (recycling?) all used up fecal despots back into its hungry bowels.

Illustrious Supplicants:
Duc de Saint-Simon,
Tristram Shandy,
Émilie du Châtelet,
Usbek and Rica,
Robert Robert Livingston—double R Livingston.

Mercury or The Dithering Dipygus

Father-mother of data-doms, ideas—*claires et distinctes*, jingos for lingo, indices of weighted whimpering, quarterly mood metrics, data-driven doldrums, scheduled spontaneity, rabbincal upspeakers, pattern makers, semantic otakus, remedial reading pulsars.

Governs deductive logic, literary science, sand-cipher generation, number magic, pattern porn, Islam (according to the heterodox author of *Picatrix*), mnemonic minarets, mimesis, synecdoche.

Rules over colloquies, contract juries, jury harmonics, metrical metamorphoses, atheism, civic body mods, mindful orgies, neonatal blueprinting, scattershot body utopias.

Patron of the programmers.

Regulates the half-life of bone-divination broth, the Mendelian "common sense" of the Ajami Private Diction.

His Mollitude in Middle Age means plea bargains,

commutation chess, dictionary detractors ("to define is to distrust").

His void portends convection (moroseness leading to paggro supernovae), neural petrifacts, data famine, backend scripting El Dorados, automated automation, housebroken highbrows, constipated solipsism, fin de siècle self-help seminars, Soviet Realism.

On Mood Metrics:

"My quarterly mood metrics, pending seasonal revisions, inform me that on average I committed suicide 1.28 times last Thursday afternoon."

On Scheduled Spontaneity:

Calendar Invite. "Astonishment in 15 (or 16?!?) minute intervals every other Thursday, 3–5 PM."

On Soviet Realism (*Chanson de geste*):

"And Boyar Murrogh fell to his knees upon the grass that was black with bourgeois blood, and the broken edge of Prole Tristram's scythe lay deep-buried in his head. And anon he leapt up as he had been mad...and so fled unto his Daimler straight-six limousine, sore squealing as he went."

His Infernal Idolaters (void worshippers):

Swinburne—"Worked with him once on a butchery project. A disappointing first contact with a man who, according to slaughterhouse gossip, claimed he had sex with an edible monkey."

Illustrious Supplicants:

Giordano Bruno,

Francois Magendie—"eyes but no ears" empiricist, mechhead.

Apocryphal Apostates:

Disraeli or Mark Twain—"lies, damn lies, and statistics."

⊕

'Awwa or The Barking Puppicules

Father-mothers of short b-ball players, bubonic fleas, sickly geniuses, undersized übermenschen, the ΦX174 virus, castrated abbesses.

Their Mollitude in Middle Age means more of the same.

Illustrious Supplicants:
Muggsy Bogues,
Antonie van Leeuwenhoek,
Héloïse—monastically castrated to appease her vengefully castrated lover Abelard,
Finland,
James Madison,
Aedes aegypti,
Giacomo Leopardi.

$\oplus$

Butayn or The Little Belly

Father-mother of levelheaded, cubby-minded (compartmentalizing) sex workers, premature food babies, surplus stomachs, persnickety thrill-seekers, lunchable lunch ladies, scrupulous death-wishers, diapered pensioners.

Fountain-father of thirst traps.

Rules over regimented satiation, adultery benchmarks, budget orgasms, the ecology of pleasure, hard gemlike phlegm, charmed flip-floppers (like Descartes, ever bumbling onto the winning side), bereavement balance.

His Mollitude in Middle Age means edible Epicureans, Darwinian rhapsodies.

On Darwinian Rhapsodies (Tennyson):
"I held it truth, with him who sings, to one clear harp in divers tones, that Men may rise on stepping-stones of their dead selves to higher things."

His void portends manic safety freaks, fanatical hand-washers, priggish pussy-parchers.

Illustrious Supplicants:
Elisabeth of Bohemia.

Supplicants in Middle Age:
Lucretius,
Walter Pater,
Tennyson.

Unintended Supplicants or Illustrious Flip-Floppers:
Descartes—conscript in the Catholic Counter-Reformation army that crushed King Frederick of Bohemia's ecumenical alliance. Later, *philosophe* and tutor-ustadh to Frederick's brilliant daughter Elisabeth, inventor of Cartesian mechanics which deals the killing blow to the earthbound power of the Catholic church.

Schrödinger Supplicants:
Leibniz—but only those doppel-Leibnizes who exist in the best of multiversal worlds.

On Bereavement Balance:
"The worst part was that every time I allowed myself to mourn, the thought of her delighted me while every delightful memory doubled me over with grief."

The Sun or The Melting Beloved

Of celestial no-fire we are told by Mandeville that "God" quenched the pyre of a woman wrongfully accused with "His" facelight (Numbers 6:24-26), transforming the burning brands into red and white roses. In their greed for roses, the townsmen, ever after, would burn all the innocent maidens they could lay their hands on, though prices remained inflated due to miracle supply volatility.

Father-mother of ruddy lips and rubies, mannequins, Aztec heart engines, immigrant melting pots, scandal mongrels.

Rules lovey-dovey volcano divers.

Regulates mass-immolation rights, the search for the Fountain of Assisted Suicide.

Its void portends cloning fads, hermit pogroms, patois detergent agents, prosthesis sharing schedules, student smelting initiatives (character refinement), teacher amalgam funding (headcount reduction).

Illustrious Supplicants:

    Hafiz,

    Phaedra,

    Paracelsus—"If she thinks a fire, she _is_ fire, if she thinks of war, she becomes a war."

The Mechanist or The Prosthetic Star

Father-mother of hand maestros, finger makers, artificers, spider bees, polymerists, effigists, handmade house mud homunculi.

    Regulator of metacarpal kinks, pet petters, wrist-lover subreddits.

Illustrious Supplicants:

    al-Jazari,

    William and Jane Morris,

    Ambroise Paré,

    Norbert Wiener.

The Vitalist or The Body Star

The "Body Star" is a registered large and small intestine donor to ailing white dwarves.

Father-mother of the body politic as body-horror film, progressive dicks (leaning left).

From: The Association of Pedagogical Pathologists

To: Tinjitan Town Hall Elders

Subject: A plea for community youth center cadavers and dissection funding.

The Argument: "Most of us know less about our own bodies than the 16th century anatomist Andreas Vesalius..."

⊕

Shaghab or The Spider Queen

Father-mother of spider moms, multitasking matriarchs, octuplets, asynchronous child swaddlers, asynchronous child paddlers (nuns and immigrant families mostly), all-seeing brood bosses, pediatric spider milk theory.

Regulator of multilegged brood control, filial anagrams, pupal puppet rearing, trauma hatcheries, dynastic credit scores.

Her Mollitude in Middle Age means scullery intrigue, chore contracts, buffer children, disciplinary hostage taking, sibling secession.

Her void portends family values as prison-building, parasite parenting, demilitarized middle sons, church mandated puberty, geriatric canneries, seraglio strangulation politics.

On Spider Moms:

Spins her web of self-esteem in ratio to the thickness of her paunch. Breeds spiderlings who measure all enormities of good and evil in rectal ratio to their silk deficient buttholes.

Illustrious Supplicants:

Tiberius,

Muqtadir.

⊕

Venus or The Body of Body Language

Father-mother of body poets, tarsa infidels, nonverbal chatterboxes, tic tutors, the lily with her cunnilingual sword, AAA lustral narrative pearls.

Ruler of epidermal jargon insemination, oratorical gesticulation, asabiyya—group feeling, international "pan" movements, carcass conglomerates, derogatory trash twerking, silent majorities, terse (amputee) gods.

Explicates the grammar of functional relationships, mass market musculature, body distortion lingo (gravitational curvature convos).

Governs the organizing principle, morphogenetic child rearing, cultural cohesiveness, electromagnetic fields, ritual ecology, mandible magic, tendon magic, the infestation of grief, autologous tear transfusion (left eye).

Organizes the color palette of qamariyya story-glass windows, hernia emojis.

Her Mollitude in Middle Age means mass handshaking, community acquired conspiracy theories, four-letter gestures, twitch tectonics, movement mores, mass democracy.

Her void portends sweat surplus, neighborly body-minders, blood man's burden, crowd pleasers, crowd pleasures, unintended altruism, density fetish (swarm syndrome), harlequin humanism, massacre democracy.

On Massacre Democracy:

"Is it democracy when six or seven leaders can nuke the world and nuke the button and nuke the finger that pressed the button in 15 minutes, but it takes 45 minutes to drive to my local polling station?"

On Density Fetishes:

Elias Canneti points out that a <u>culling</u> only strengthens the crowd. Culling is a morale booster. An odds booster. The enemy has wasted energy killing <u>one</u> when they might have killed them all.

On Imperial Transfusion Sympathy (Blood Man's Burden):

COIN 3rd edition Rule Book.

Pre Burden Campaign: Victory Points = (+d10 * body bags) + $\log_e$(Suppositional Body Count)

Post Burden Campaign: Victory points = $\log_e$(Suppositional Body Count) - (+d10 * body bags)

Illustrious Supplicants:

Qin Guan,

Averroes,

Galina Ulanova,

Cao Xueqin,

Spengler,

Zuhra.

Illustrious Apostates:

Isaac Babel,

Condorcet,

Kawakami Gensai.

Saturn or The Vndercover Memory Massager

Father-Mother of cranks, paranoid databases, the redacted freedom fighters called "Codon," gangster-cop symbiotes, schizophrenic public keys, subcutaneous police informants, algorithmically generated historians, patchwork memory artists, surrogate baby bump bombers, cultic cat parasites, aerosol profiling preppers (COINTEL selfie powder-camera dispersal nozzles), gene phishers, programmable whistleblowers.

Governs random anarchist generators, saliva ciphers, civic cage fighting, conspiracy factories, pod people podcasts, holographic hospitals, prescription creed switching, pirated organ modeling torrents (OM6 fuzzy decompression/decomposition format), unidentified flying fucks given, historical astrology, side-hustle mass grave digging, the occultation of Imams.

Regulator of teenage swarm culture, the rigorous biochemistry of hell ("their skin regrows without miracles"), deep state mitosis, message molly, the family values vaccine, cheapfake pharmacology, penal anemia, inspiration glands, municipal gaslighting, locust (nutrition) festivals.

Obstetrician for digestive cell replacement, reproductive cannibalism, regurgitation babies, annihilation/apotheosis cultures.

On Locust (Nutrition) Festivals:

"Eat the rich. Looters will be deemed rich and added to the menu."

On Municipal Gaslighting:

Wherein the pigs gaslight protesters by incinerating their uniforms, demolishing police stations and prisoners, repainting patrol cars and getting plastic surgery. "Police reform? What police?"

Prop Prophet of scriptural white noise.

His Mollitude in Middle Age means patriotic cannabis, orthodox bank balances, loyalty laxatives, lonely chatbot spammers, chatbot cartels, cane sugar pedigree intrigue, civic rebranding algorithms, nucleic grammar reform, laboratory cities, swarm snitching, lexicon rehab, mufti mammary mandates, the radical partisans called "Codon," offshore orphan supply chain AI, fission freestate fables, ballot-stuffing clones, alleged allergy seasons, counterinsurgent pollen, knockoff bankers, tranquility toothpaste (trank paste) deniers, model minority fermentation programs, redaction mania, encryption dispersal syndrome, decryption derangement disorder, monomer monetization.

His void portends afterschool cannibal programs, baby depletion crisis, strategic ovary reserve, insemination quotas, reproductive stimulus (welfare) drones, fertility viruses, organ donor (excavation) orgies, syndicate germ surveillance, incel mitosis, deepfake hurricanes, illegal alien abduction, synaptic black sites, Intersectional ~~White~~ Man's Burden, the terrorist group

"Codon," query dementia, hydraulic despotism, the social synod, subdermal sleeper agents, genealogy brigades, crowdfunded drug wars.

On Genealogy Brigades:

According to the historian Paul Johnson "accurate genealogies, secretly circulated, were a form of subversive literature."

Illustrious Suppliants:

The Imamite Sleeper Agent (Legitimist Mole) Shalmaghani,
The Mameluke Lion Slayer Bint Hushang,
Alexander Pope,
John Dee,
Hippolytus,
The Priest Eater Bar Yaqub—in prison the Radiant Imaad, by special ecclesiastical dispensation, allows him to wear a kitschy "Free Bar Yaqub" T-shirt,
Guicciardini.

The Junction (Ménage) of Mercury and Venus:

Co-Consuls of skeptical passion projects, dating ghostbusting initiatives, defunded smash sessions, gravity entitlers, machine-mind kabbalah, *relâche des sens* or sensual repose, capsule demographies (ingestible nobodies or no-minder biographies).

Illustrious Suppliants:

Ada—non-binary codon coils, La Infanta de Princess of Parallelograms, The Enchantress of Number.
Mind-body Mary Astell—the Cartesian feminist.

The Vlemic Jupiter or The Judicial Microbe

Father-mother of the growing power, agronomists, dryland
ecologists, union leaders, city repletion metrics, frontier farmers,
urologists, charity crusaders, virologists, nuclear physicists,
bioweapon engineers.

Governs the duration of empires, the biology of religious laws,
famine fury conversion, handicap resource wars, DNA replication
errors, gestation cycles, man on man colonization, housing
recombination projects, the half-life of goof juice taboos, nuclear
proliferation, crowd congealment velocity, the epidemiology
of celibacy, virile charisms, *le grande derange* ("the scheduled
schizophrenia and cosmetic surgery of crowds"), supermarket
growth hormones, berserker feedback loops.

Regulates ancestral sperm worship, disaster damage,
All-American (Chinese) welfare factories, Noah syndrome,
millenarian malignancy armies, unplanned mother-parts
infestation, loyalty in plague times.

On Loyalty in Plague Times (Montaigne):
"On the contrary, after that I never again left his side."
His Mollitude in Middle Age means eruption dysfunction,
earthquake fatigue and seismic hormone replacement therapy,
fallopian blockouts (union and non-union), density panic.

It void portends neonatal nativism, GMO grocer guerillas, the
body politic as tumescent body-horror film, urban decomposition
poisoning, doppelgang warfare, fertilizer wars, data nativism,
database table secession, test tube baby bombers, asexually
reproducing farmland, splinter sect sons, copycat viruses.

Illustrious Supplicants:
Daniel O'Connell (The Emancipator),
Norman Borlaug,
Sun Myung Moon,
Spolverini (and his sentient rice poems),
The Aneedee ultra leader Bar Sinjaq Miskeen and his peasant
"Dignity Harvests",

Peter The Hermit,
Edward Teller,
Billy Graham,
Goya.

The Junction (Ménage) of Shaghab and Jupiter

Governs historical astrology, the physiology of law, blubbery
Oversouls, the long run, board-certified imposter syndrome, the
broad view, anticipatory anthropology, decline and fall dogmas,
the butter (churn) of wisdom, dementia debt deductions, polity
mitosis, cultural organisms, roadkill geographers, Darwinian
cartographers.

On Darwinian Cartographers:
  "For as Geography without History seemeth a carkasse
without motion, so History without Geography wandreth as a
Vagrant without a certaine Habitation."

On the Oversoul(Oswald Spengler):
  "Paris called the Germans Allemands in 1814, Prussians in
1870, Boches in 1914—in other circumstances three distinct
peoples might have been supposed to be covered by these names."

Illustrious Supplicants:
  Spinoza,
  Bar Hebraeus,
  Emerson,
  The Radical Mitochondriac Bint Hassiba Slimane,
  Ibn Khaldun.

Mars or The Ravishing Rick Rude

Father-mother of town founders, religious third forcers
(Ecumenicists, Erasmians, Unitarians, Freemasons, Hallajians),
affable dumb-doms, teambuilding sucrose chefs, techie tantrum
troubleshooters, Unitarian chat aggregators, interintestinal
ingénues, big dick energy humanists.

Rules all attracting powers, conciliatory circumcisions, zeal,
charisma and charisms, oratory, ecumenicalism, coagulants, caking
agents, commutation committees.

Regulates the average duration of panic attacks, the silent
treatment, bottomless brunch diplomacy, nondenominational
chromatid crossover, coagulation squads, girl on girl ovations, boy
on boy mothering.

On Coagulation Squads:
"In the land of the bleeders the coagulator is king.
Commercial tagline: 'Give 'em a thicky instead of a pricky.'"
Matchmaker of conjugal volcano jumpers, affinities, cosmic
eagle eggs.

On Cosmic Eagle Eggs:
As "eagle wings in the egg presuppose air," so Newton hatches
apples, stars, spooky gravitons, so soldiers are "Shield Bastards"
(which seems, at first, an antique metaphor) and thus the glory-
name of the petcheneg swaddled in conniving god-skin fathers.

His Mollitude in Middle Age produces neighborhood
coarseness, volcanic flatulators, gamesbound intimacy, religious
water balloon wars, flammable papier-mâché Unitarians,
intrigue, the Inquisition in every office, human resource manuals,
lickspittles, Good Samaritan hiring quotas, anti-loneliness
crusaders.

On Gamesbound Intimacy:
"It's always prudent to feign a male sportsball fetish to
preempt violence. The modern man still needs his Darwinian
pressure valves."

It void portends demagoguery, mob hysteria, consumption conscripts, sectarian saturation bombing, treachery templates, human service atrocity, invasive empathy algorithms, conjugal leprosy, social frankness ("drooling mouth policies"), the will to harmony, co-ed intramural crucifixion leagues, bereavement ablation surgery, estrangement exterminators.

Fear the Fox Bite. Under this star, the fox is always rabid.

Illustrious Supplicants:
Shakh-i-Nabat (The Branch of Candy),
Sulkhan-saba Orbeliani (The Book of Pleasing Lies),
Frantz Fanon,
Erasmus of Rotterdam,
Confucius.

⊕

The Junction (Ménage) of Mars and Saturn

Presides over the annual Independence Day arms buildup, altruistic vampires (compulsive blood givers), paramilitary hedgehogs, freedom of intelligence requests, declassified youth counselors, public enemy puppet shows, anarchist pops (mango, tutti frutti, crystal moth and amatol), blackmail discounts, cute Confucian autocrats, whisker plot plots and beard graphs, fake mustache crutches, false flag self-help seminars.

⊕

The Dragon

Intensifies good or bad luck.
Father-mother of incendiary cigars.
Rules over shipwreck bloopers, pratfalls, lottery ticket pickpockets, taxable inheritances, guest right cannibals, xenophobic antibodies.

Illustrious Supplicants:
    Charles Babbage,
    Ibn Battuta,
    Walter Raleigh,
    John Law.

The Anti-Dragon

Intensifies good or bad fucks.

Illustrious Supplicants:
    Neutral Milk Hotel,
    George Sand (Amantine Lucile Aurore Dupin),
    Li Shizhen—compiler of snake wine aphrodisiac recipes.

Neptune or The Tough Crack to Nut

Father-mother of placid philosophers, pixelated graphic designers, terraphobic skyscraper builders, drama-queen deniers.

Rules over restraint, molecular proportion, amino acid awareness, gamete greaser restraint, emotional field stripping, LEGO intellection.

Her void portends popular emission diets, mass market monkishness, viral asceticism, policy wonks, morality pandemics, death by stock market.

Illustrious Supplicants:
    Oliver Byrne,
    Montesquieu,
    Bertha Crawford Hubbard,
    Chris Ware,
    Grotius,

Plotinus:
    Owen Jones.

⊕

Al-Bnaat or The Doubler Daughters

Doublers of all their father-mothers' influence. Averagers of two
or more incompatible adverse destinies.

Regulator of redundant tautologies, surgery to correct the
complications of surgery.

Rules over megaphones, bisected doublespeak, EDM hearing
aids, moebius feedback loops, Nietzschean clockmakers, surplus
skyminders , harmonic inseminators ("her operatic daughters
will burst, in vitro, from her lover's throats"), warbling chiffchaffs,
ululating fitna inciters, pulpating fitna incisors, laborer-saving
devices.

Illustrious Supplicants:
    Hieronymus Fabricius ab Aquapendete,
    Georg Ernst Stahl—mufti of molecular motive fire,
    Xavier Bichat—cult of sensibility.

⊕

Al-Aql or The Active Intellect

The stars are love, they love themselves. Like dogs, they chase
their own beloved butts, revolving always back to start.

Illustrious Supplicants:
    Al-Farabi,
    Aquinas.

Rejected Supplicants:
    All brown nosing naturalists.

⊕

The Seven Thrones or The Seven Exaltations of Poetry

6) ???.

Illustrious Supplicants:
    Jaami.

⊕

The Eye of Azra

> "Gaze, till Gazing out of Gazing."
>   —Jaami

⊕

Supplicatory Voyeurs:
    William Hunter—author of *The Anatomy of the Human Gravid Uterus Exhibited in Figures,*
    Marie Van Brittan Brown,
    Dr. Hiromi Shinya—co-inventor of the colonoscope,
    Stubbins Ffirth—membership under review, an edge case for ingesting his own digestion after failing to catch yellow fever from stealing and eating his patient's bile,
    Walter Jackson Freeman II—lobotomist, showman, unwitting devotee of Montesquieu's dictum, "Professions appear ridiculous only in proportion to the professional gravity adopted: a doctor would be less absurd if his dress were more cheerful and if, while killing his patients, he jested pleasantly."

⊕

Farhad or The Hag of Darkness

Father-Mother of plastic flower mothers, obsolete genies.
   Regulator of livershare apps, peer-to-peer peglegs,
polyurethane perfume, pentimento pec implants.
   Auctioneer of secondhand Jodorowsky poop, vivisected
messiah relics, regurgitated snow droppings.

Adulterous Supplicants:
   Jaami,
   Shibli.

⊕

Bittacus or The Talking Starship

Zookeepers of emotional werewolves.

⊕

So-102 or The Meh and The Shrug

Recycler of thunderstones (ceraunias), abaddirs, cardiac blood
fountains, funeral rites, indifferent eulogists, trash compactors.

Hobbies In Middle Age:
   Supernova watching.

Retirement Reading List:
   Porson's *History of Human Folly in Five Hundred Volumes*,
   Adam's *Defence of the Constitutions*,
   Nuri's *Aphorism's for Strange Flowers*,
   Bar Nadim's *Patchwork Compendium*.

⊕

Sagittarius A or The Hole in the Hole

> "Nothing on nothing, all is Nothing—Enough."
> —Farid Ad-din Attar

⊕

Father-mother of roundabout influencers, roundabout liberators, The 77 Invisible (Occulted) Do-Gooders Who Keep the Nukes from Going Boom, anecdotal diplomacy, collateral puppification campaigns, sheepish caudillos.

Its Mollitude in Middle Age:
    Anal-attentive free markets, domesticated generalissimo cages, pasteurized ("retired") elder statesmen, private service communes, allegorical freedom of information tie-in novels.
    Its void portends nothingness, neverness.

Illustrious No-Minders:
    Nikita Khrushchev,
    Stu Ungar,
    Oblomov,
    William Lindsay Graham—"No Address. No Phone. No Business. No Money. Retired,"
    Simon Bolivar.

THE MOVTH OF THE WORD

The Islamic philosopher Averroes once wrote that God, the Eternal, did not create the world. He <u>knows</u> the world, and because God only believes the truth, the world exists to justify God's honesty.

Against this Averroes's predestined enemy—the destroyer of philosophers, Ghrazali— denies that self-made things could live up to the standards of a Perfect Being. He recounts the story of a decapitated criminal who, daily denying the atomic nature of God, subsequently seeded children, prayed, fasted, and fed the poor until the All-Knowing noticed the man was dead and rescinded the cadaver's good deeds.[50] To justify this divine ruthlessness, Ghrazali lies. He writes, "The man failed to earn his accidental life." Which I take to mean that he had done only the believer's bare minimum.[51] This hardly explains why God condescends to spare you, the lukewarm reader, or I—the most unreliable of atheists.

---

[50] The heresiarch Hudayj accuses god of rescinding the man's beneficiaries.
[51] Less, in fact, for on the way to join the Meccan caravan he paused to bury his wife near Jeddah and missed the hajj. At that moment god, sensing an opening, was able to erase him with a clear conscience.

I recall Hafiz, the Sufi poet-mystic, asked:

"Did love come first or the beloved? I met a shadow on the wall, the sun arose to project it. Blind, the darkling I adored. My eyes swelled to fill their sockets. Behind me something leopard—with braided pubes, tattooed nips, and perfume tresses—ripped my unlikely arm off. My hands erupted from their stumps to paint her with invented colors."

Four years later, the teenage Hafiz sees the subject of these verses, Shakh-e Naba, for the first time. She would not requite his worship. Could not, for he—a baker's drudge—was too poor to introduce himself.[52] Unlike Dante's Beatrice, she declines to star in his poetry. Husayn Ibn Nasr Al-Wazzan Al-Balkhi—the ra'wi and disciple of Jaami—says enigmatically that Shakh-e Naba woke, like Eve, on the first day of creation, from a centuries long sleep. While the academician Simon Rosenthal suspects Hafiz invented his muse through the "camouflage of judicious omission." Elsewhere, in his much deplored *Chronography of Persia,* Rosenthal insinuates that Shakh-e Naba lurks to one day ambush some lucky, predestined reader.

Of predestiny, the following:

I think I have detected in the biography of Hafiz a prefiguration of Rumi—jurist, poet, rival mystic. That Rumi died a century before Hafiz is hardly relevant.

For the Sufis, all men are contemporaries in a chronology only slightly less fantastic than the radiometric time of the paleontologists. Descendant. Ancestor. Identicular marbles in the maw of the hungry-hungry hippo of Eternity or parasites residing in an infinite intestine without stomach or rectum, beginning or end.

---

[52] A bijoux indiscrets (suggestive trinket), surreptitiously deposited in the lady's boudoir, was the socially approved introduction.

Both mystics often recited drunk. What Rumi said of Shams Tarbrizi—that spirit-brother which his jealous son and disciples assassinated at the door of their favorite tavern—would better have applied to Hafiz. "None was ever more shit-faced and less distraught."[53]

Only when Rumi drank could he explain to himself why he enjoyed life so much more than other people or utter mutterances like the following. "We disfigure ourselves and discover our lovers somehow perfect."

Both had sexy thoughts about God, though one was dom, one was sub. Rumi was uninterrupted maleness, the Muslim ideal. The merkin above was as hairy as the merkin below. While Hafiz was soft enough for the spankings to bruise.

Either one might have agreed with the father of Christian scholasticism, Thomas Aquinas, who said that "God first created sex and <u>then</u> men and women to enjoy it." Certainly both knew that desires should <u>always</u> be indulged precisely because they could never be satisfied until that fated union, reunion, with the All-Sufficient.

---

[53] Compare Martial's envious line. "He deceives who thinks Acerra reeks of yesterday's wine. Acerra always drinks until morning."

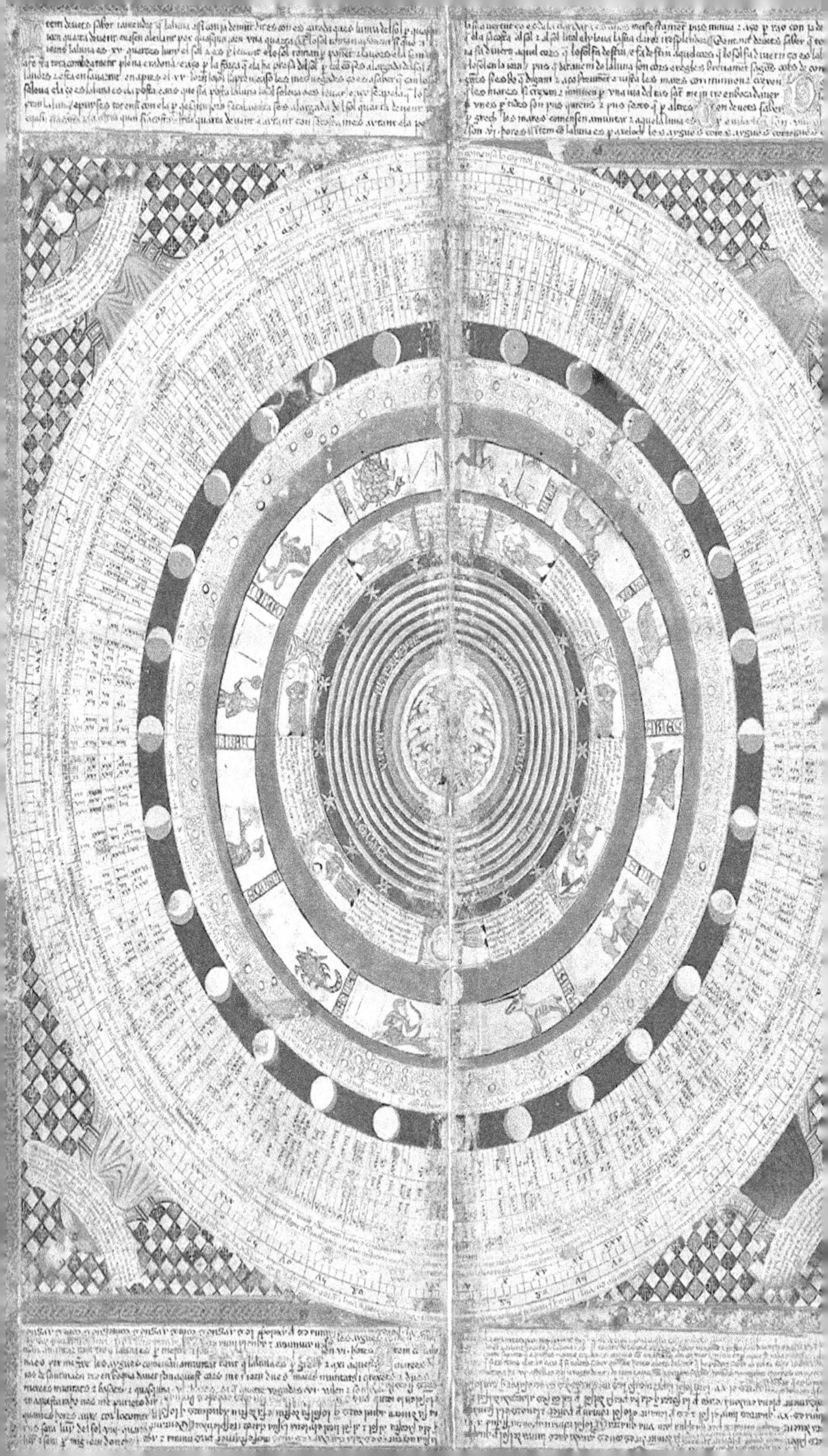

THE WORLD ABOVE THE MOON

The Moon Above the Moon

On night one thousand and two[54] of the *Aboriginal Compendium*, Sinbad the Landsman challenges Sinbad the Sailor to justify his wealth. Their secret affinity is never explored, other than to set the star-crossed drudge against the undeserving prodigal.

What is marvelous are not the tales of the Sailor—"The Thinking World," "The Monomatic Bird," "The Chaplet of Wisdom," "The Hermit Harem," or "The Spiral Minaret of Hands"—but the parsimony of the storyteller in presenting a mystery he forgets to solve. From the moment the Sailor begins his story, the Landsman is dismissed from its pages though not, perhaps, from existence.[55]

---

[54] The anonymous tale-teller justifies this surplus night, a violation of the more common title, through the careless implementation of Nietzsche's doctrine of Eternal Redundance.

[55] One suspects, idly, that their proximity should have erased both men from the fable.

Dehappenstance

So that the seed twice bestowed by a visible charm might be
propagated among all mankind, Sinbad the Landsman murders
Sinbad the Sailor and assumes his fortune.

The Sailor had taken a vow of celibacy—a literal castrato
according to one tradition—for in his travels he had learned
to despise mankind and did not wish to increase its numbers.
Bar Urqud, working from episcripts long since sterilized,
optimistically adds. "Neither did he dare improve, by a single
letter, the perfect Book of Creation."

The Landsman pays dowry to 10,000 women of proven
fertility and makes it his business to adopt vagrants, a vast wasiya
legacy of heirs whose vow of promiscuity they continue to impose
on their descendants down to the present era.

The Birth of Yesterday

According to that most faithful witness Bint Hassiba Slimane—
who told it to Bint Rabi'a in the year of her manumission—our
descendants, traveling through ever more hostile cosmos, passed
beyond the sphere in which a plurality of men could survive.
Entire populations died, innumerable generations in fact, for
medicine had made men otherwise immortal. The survivor,
shrifting through vacant hells, without even the stifled screams
of The Damned to absolve her guilt, evolved in accordance with
the bottleneck law ("life is a sluggish edge case of death"). Her
daughter gives birth to her posthumous mother, as Eve in Pre-
Adamic times grew from the stillborn gore of Eve.[56]

---

[56] There is a patriarchal parallel in Cinaethon, who tells how our starving
father Odysseus devoured the castaway Ithacans, parents of his forgotten
parents, and is killed in turn by his bastard Telegonus, who erupts from
the recombinant entrails of the kinslayer. We think also of the general
theory of telegony as reformulated by the Gnostics. "Whom the adulterer
loves shall be born again her son."

THE GARDEN OF FIRE

Man, whose roots are hellfire.
> —The Book of Weeds (forgery)

☩

Everything that really counts is veiled,
testimony and documents obscure, deeds
design, disfigure and deform."
> —Paul Valéry

☩

This Patois of Silence

The Ajami Private Diction is our Darwinian hadith, contradictory
codons and argumentative genes. A mutating database of
traditions which may congeal briefly into gametic fiqh to condole
human catastrophe[57] but impossible to codify; facts, not petrifacts,
mercurial beliefs which will never freeze into adamantium creeds,
turbulent riverings of sentience not glacial apothegms, axioms and
fallacies dividing, seceding, like the Body Politic of our Sanhadjan
Mitochondriarchy. No two permutations of hadith are allowed to
agree. No juridical school can claim supernal authority. All holy

---

[57] <u>Human</u>. Are there other types of catastrophe?

writ, written by or ghostwritten for the Divinity, could be twisted
into single helices. Some Sanhadjans believe that to unravel the
first 10 million twists of the AJPD would unravel reality.[58]

The AJPD is a zealot zoology. Polymer-proselytes and
monomer-witnesses professing every gospel or perjury,
every charter for human dignity or eugenic screed, every
recombinatorial manifesto or gibbering idiocy, every plea for
social uplift or philanthropic brainwashing, every infallible book
of historical astrology, every dietary fad or anatomical rhapsody,
every lucid corollary or almanac of insanity.[59] The AJPD does not

---

[58] The emaciated hologram Bar Hallaj, no otaku for reality, has desecrated
rigorously and experimentally and declares it impossible, reporting. "The
Ajami Private Diction, repository of all fates, including the fate of the
AJPD, may omit nothing except how to destroy the AJPD."

[59] "Insanity as vaccine," according to Bint Eshon, an opinion which
unanimously prevented her election to the Lyceum, the panel refusing
to even read the addendum attached to her application explaining that
the AJPD was meant to "fossilize fallibility, not cacophony." All her life
Bint Eshon's brother-sister artists treated her with astonishing disloyalty,
pretending to acclaim her suicidal pursuit of excellence during the Ornati
fad for aesthetic martyrdom while slurping insinuendos and retching
nauseously over "her secretions in prose and mucosal poetry" to the
delight of their vicious toyminder sponsors, even before the worm began
to turn, fusing, docile, with the Social Mush the moment the Synods had
secured their transitory hegemony over cultural patronage on the back
of the Zenata Mob whose moral nutrition mania, mandatory optimism
and senility decrees elevated a bestial longevity over the Sanhadjan
inversion principle of mitosis (cell death without death) and infinitesimal
immortality.

The critic Bar Junayd abandoned her as a favor to the editor of *Sleep*—a
powerbroker in publishing but, vis-à-vis the social elite, a no-minder
pimp who had done no more than primp and grease his pet critic into
the fashionable Arrondissement Jusham, during a period when every
skyminder sect snubbed Junayd as a surgeon snubs a benignant cyst.
During Bint Eshon's show trial for pornographic pessimism—a brazen
inquisition into the artist's ancient faith in Tragedy and Catharsis—
Junayd wrote hedging articles expressing "the opinion of a favorite who
will recant on his deathbed" as Bar Huthayl, channeling La Bruyère
scolding the toadies of the OG Sun King, aptly sneering. Junayd evaded

disdain tautology. There is a golden chain of the highest reliability in my personal-hermetic AJPD, each monomer repeating, word for word, the same argument in favor of the doctrine of Eternal Redundancy. In odium theologicum what matters is victory, not the interchangeability of each side's arguments.

⊕

Homolog or Gonadal Typography

In the margins I have interred cadaver-effigies of our Conscript Fathers unraveling in amino acid arabesques, ACGT dissolving into gonadal glyphs.

The glyphs in the left margin, the Paralog, decrypt at the touch of a Sanhadjan[60] citizen or mawla-adoptee infested with the

---

any discussion of the specific charges against the artist in favor of oblique manifestos in defense of Art, allowing the Cacophonists (to which sect, the aforementioned editor was a regular donor) to smear Bint Eshon as a Squelch, the most perverse of Quietists, adorers of that abhorred patois of silence, gratuitously concluding his final article by gutlessly regretting, without recanting, the scathing <u>tone</u> of those lampoons against the Cacophonists he had written as a "pupating firebrand" and generally selling his former idol to the idol smashers. The Cacophonists... whose methods of controversy include eviscerations of enemy effigies as "allegorical pressure valve" and cheerleading activist porcelain bombers (though quick to denounce the "catastrophic confluence of coincidence" which occurred on 17th Majnuun, 309 W.E.—they refused to excommunicate the killers until three weeks after the fourth fugitive bomber was caught *in conflagrante delicto*). Their greater hajj is a kissing tour of all 87 million mouths of Cacophony, even those mouths which slander other mouths as untrustworthy or like to snack on human lips in between screaming 87 million *malaahims*. Cacophony—the controversial || incontrovertible Ajami <u>Public</u> Diction, a civic innovation patriotically digesting Sanhadjan bodies and blending (or flattening) the dissonant destinies of our private-hermetic AJPDs. A vanilla martyrdom is to transcribe the shrieking vedas and veneratiae of Mouth #38574 through Mouth #42838 until deaf.

[60] In cadaver cant—<u>Sanhadjan Akayim</u>, the fabricated sons of our castrato fathers.

AJPD. The Ortholog is a mutating mausoleum of trivia meant to
amuse or placate the prefabricated foreigner.

⊕

Ortholog 1: Phenotype

> "And late to fullness grows the birth that
> shall last as long as earth."
> —The Shropshire Lad

⊕

Phenotype is the circus showcase of genes: a pauper's beak,
ornamental teats, the villainous baritone of the financier Ibn Furat
in the operatic "Wheel of Fiscal Suffering," our body's fierce or
flippant strategy against tuberculosis. As with our bestial prefab
DNA, so with our civic genes,[61] primal phenotypes mixing with
those father-mothered by the AJPD to lurk unseen except to
retinas too specialized for our captains of industry to lucratively
breed. The phenotypes of the AJPJD can go extinct or speciate
into a zoology, ample and struggling, the Epidermal Jihad between
phenotypes mirroring the Subdermal Jihad between sectarian
hadith (strife without slaughter, fitness without fitna-eugenics or
collateral martyrs).

Many will read this carefully. Whether with premeditated
scorn or sympathy, many will misunderstand completely. The
AJPD supplies no auguries or wobbling waveform prophecies.
Neither do we Sanhadjans waft through analytic data dreams
or tranquilize ourselves like Sister Sibyllines as Bar Huthayl
claims slanderously. Instead, there is a kind of annexation of our
attention, akin to that which Parasite Saints spread according to
the tactics of their Tariqa-Orders, ambushing and embracing,
while cooing charismatically, their sweat intruding intravenously

---

[61] Civic is the central adjective of Sanhadjan fabrication and gonadology,
the cipher-key which our Conscript Fathers bequeathed to us with a mix
of benignity and fatalism.

into the pores of new initiates or rueful renegades, afflicting them with an accumulating <u>disposition</u> towards erotic mysticism (sex == fusion with the Undivided Supreme).

Who will accuse me of reckless analogy? Lately it seems that no Sanhadjan can elicit understanding, instead of universalist cant and hangdog sympathy, without being accused of feeding our enemies. Are we that naive? The Anti-Sanhadjan is to conspiracy theories what the locust is to calories. The lack of all evidence against us proves our genius for criminality, couriers for a chromosomal disease, puppeteers of human beings, an infectious world cabal of gametic fedayeen.

Yet we too accuse, more viciously because of our inseparable (I almost wrote <u>insuperable</u>) self-intimacy. Assuming universal suspicion, the Sanhadjan émigré suspects everybody, preemptively persecuting his persecutors, or else he grovels and appeases, snorkeling in the toxic slime of other people's bigotries or else sinking and mutating, an irradiated mishmash of toyminder vices, Sanhadjan caste arrogance and ghetto anxiety. On the dissection table an anatomist of genius would exhaust himself trying to categorize the hostile species which contributed their glands and orifices to this flagellating freak. Even the reconciliation between the Mitochondriarchy and our Diaspora—those pliable Sanhadjans who excel at <u>taqiyya</u>, the culling of all dispositions bred from the AJPD which might incite persecution—has not bestowed inner peace. The successful émigré sees in her rediscovered sister-indigène flaws she once forgave herself for as <u>immigrant</u> eccentricities, rather than rejoice at her readoption into the wider Sanhadjan family, she succumbs to genetic fatality, mimicking the mood of our isolationist *ultras* and their nexus of convenience with the LMP (Leechcraft Minority Parties). Yet in fairness we must admit that repatriation and heritage tours cannot change the fact that in a world teeming with undiscovered sympathy (and unsuspecting sympathizers), crevices still exist where a pogrom is nevertheless happening. That the *ultras* spend so much time scaremongering and scapegoating the *évolué* (the transcendent cousins of the antique *umanisti*) does not imply that the latter have achieved anything. Who hasn't read that despicable forgery *The Book of Weeds*,[62] *first smuggled out of the satellite trauma center of the Akhuan Nursing League and made known to a world resolved, nil admirari*, to be shocked by nothing yet with a magnetic appeal to skyminders bored by the humdrum perversions of hole and nose.[63] In this absentminded nurse's copy[64]—inaugural but inaugurating <u>what</u> exactly, even our bleakest historical astrologers are too scared to <u>see</u>—the following words are underlined in double carmine bars. "So said Bar Bajjah, the Gardener of Fire: 'Whereas the obstinate are weeds in a Paradise where none but flames should ripen.'"[65]

Ortholog 2: Cadaver Cant

Its sister text, *The Book of Mold*, is so outlandish that even the most shameless paranoiac will deny its existence lest he scare off more mellow fellow travelers. Conversely, the one surefire way of identifying a brother "weed puller"—so called because they pretend to use our own terror tactics against us—is to misquote one of the book's many heinous aphorisms and see if the other person can resist pulling you aside and correcting you.

---

[62] Also referred to in Anti-Sanhadjan circles as the "Whisper Book" or "The Book of Hushes."

[63] These skyminders would appeal to publicity minded Ordini (institutional) conservatives and *Delicato* moderates looking to scapegoat some perverts, though the feebler Ordini would be tempted to play both sides of the field.

[64] She claimed to forget who had lent her the book.

[65] Garden of Fire == AJPD. Weeds == Prefab genes. Filler words like <u>prefabricated</u>, though enraging the otakus for rage, have become, for most Sanhadjans, mere sounds shorn of all ancestral animosities. In the same way the epithet "gardener" has come to be used liturgically among militant anti-Sanhadjans (the "Gardener" Bar Bajjah, Bar Sanjil, etc.), symbiotic as Homer's "<u>Divine</u> Patroclus" and "<u>wine-dark</u> sea," the idiot's furious incantation transcending vocabulary.

Paralog 1: Our Apocryphal Enemies

For decades[66] our gnostic intelligence agencies have buried secrets like prankster paleontologists with an endless supply of "dinosaur" bodies, in the hope that our apocryphal enemies will re-anatomize these as BEASTS. As of yet, our enemies prefer to cremate these as rancid red herrings.[67]

In the same vein, our authorized domestic "leaks" are terrifying only in their ability to constipate our journalists, indigestible in content and putrid in portent, inducing nothing but hemorrhoids or dry heaves.

The Twisted Helices

When my cells stop dividing, my body dies. Mitochondriarchy dies when Sanhadjans lose the right to divide. When ijma'a consensus fails, fitna-fission proceeds. The secessionists polymerize (transcribe) the Ajami Public Diction, the civic oracle of their parent chaitya,[68] obeying the fiqh-decrees derived from this constitutional clone for a prescribed length of time (The Eight Year Law or the "Placental Pandects," as some cheerfully defame it in the bugminder patois melange) until the neonatal chaitya-cell matures. Mature, each chaitya is free to differentiate itself—in other words to ornament their ordained gestation in acid arabesques—whether by placid reform or le grande dérange.

---

[66] "A blip and a wink in the long-range radar of being," Atabeg-Ascendant Bar Muzaffar assures us. "Attrition on the geological timescale is the surest road to victory."

[67] Meanwhile (lurking amidst the diaspora which Sanhadjan intelligence patronizes without protecting) the multicultural Anti-Sanhadjan sect L'Etranger continues to flourish. These Aboriginal Strangers are professionally or tactically enraged at finding themselves guests in their own home and their Sanhadjan "houseguests" playing the host.

[68] Chaitya in the patois melange alludes to a shrine for godless homunculi.

If a <u>deranged</u> (for the special Sanhadjan implications of this word, see Bar Juzjani's Lexicon) chaitya attacks the citizens of another chaitya or tries to subvert their Ajami <u>Public</u> Diction, the Consensus Army acts like a white blood cell to crush the virus.

Reverence means to surpass the Master.[69]

Our Conscript Fathers bred the Body Politic to be a work of art.[70] Fragmentation is our descendant craft, so long to learn in a life so short, as the degeneration of a character was once the craft of the novelist.

Paralog 2: A Screed Against Compassionate Dictionaries

Is there more flagrant proof that humanitarian limits on war are a sham than the widespread use of porcelain suicide bombers, with their high-end explosive organs and posh shrapnel?[71]

---

[69] During their coming-of-age party, Sanhadjan children of the founding, embryonic chaityas are required to present their commonplace strands and to teach (or reteach) the aboriginal codons of Mitochondriarchy, Ijma'a Consensus and Gametic Fiqh, to their elders in a manner suggested by the sectarian consensus of their private-hermetic AJPD. In the hinterlands this practice has lapsed in favor of what some ulcerating geezers in high office call "malignant evangelism." Wanderlust combines with the cosmopolitan lure of the Akhuan refugee skyminders to spur our young, like colonizing single cells, in a fervent dispersion of Mitochondriarchy well beyond the terminal membrane (ghraya-extremity) prescribed by our Conscript Fathers. This snapping of the synaptic bond, more violent for being voluntary, stands in sharp contrast to the diaspora of their great grandmothers who in their nomad songs always lament the Great Derangement as a cataclysm.

[70] Dante's New Flesh erupting from the recombinant entrails of the kinslayer and the stillborn gore of Eve.

[71] The Conciliation Committee goofed when they tried to domesticate war by taming the warriors. The disastrous effect was to turn honest murderers into hypocritical euthanasiasts or professional martyrs who bear all the guilt of culling the herd, cringing, if not crying, when their dilettante citizens force them to inflict politics by other means (i.e. torture) on collateral victims.

The etiquette of the bomb makers, dynastic mom-and-pop shops all, is as exquisite as the manners of an antique daimyo towards his hostage vassals. The bomb makers are proud of their strict caste quotas and advertise that the skyminder to toyminder to bugminder body count will eventually even out (no-minders don't count). When one reads that the minimum blast radius is 18 haath, these hereditary taboos seem as outmoded as formal declarations of war. The bomb makers would do better to disgrace their ancestors than to abuse the gullibility of their customers (our new "allies" included).

[Insert here -> a typographic carnage-collage, the letters "A," "L," and "T" disemboweled, the other letters "chiseled" into the page by the force of the blast.]

⊕

Edicts of the Dithering Heart

...More often, when a truce is called between our sectarian genes, they express themselves ecumenically, an adulterated phenotype which results in a dithering disposition[72] or statistical repulsion, a stratigraphic shingling of the peroneal nerve, a rapture recreated, unscrupulously, in memory, muscle spasms like continental flesh tectonics, an itch which breeds, a cautionary gurgling in the throat or gagging on inauspicious words, an eruption of stomach acid, an aeration of blood cells with supernal air, as though tiny seraphim and cherubim were shuttling oxygen to and from your lungs, the instinctive tug of some glandular steering wheel away from the seven lucid passionettes—imperceptible punctures of the heart— towards those same tempestuous passions that burned Troy down and drove Achilles to drag Hector around the battlefield like a big game trophy, the same desecration-urge that sparked the Akhuan "Social War," the god-skinned petcheneg teaming up with the colonial Metis they'd spent eight years slaughtering against a

---

[72] For the peculiar Sanhadjan implications of this word, see Bar Juzjani's Lexicon.

Dawla-Empire which only 20 years ago seemed ready to annex the planets,[73] a chafing like walking barefoot cross the kunker limestone gravel paths of the Hamajee Veldt, that neonatal ooze our single-cell fallacies and convictions crawl out of, pipettes of predestination squirting into the bewildering petri dish of human entropy, a plucking at the spider membrane, the defensive tissue bands forestalling brain damage, like the "Nocturnal Twang of St. Bizarre," a harp which up to the present day still warns the Gamareyni nuns of creeping death.

The More Popular Monsoons

...it is true. It is a factory churning out optimistic hormones and retcon moods. But if it is gauche to alter facts, after the fact, some deft cosmetic surgery (whether amending faces or feels) is justifiable to safeguard the infallibility of public opinion

Ortholog 3: Sidereal Glands

The organs which occasionally congeal as a result of the beneficent gene snipping/shifting of the AJPD are always vestigial, they serve no managerial, archival or motor function except cosmologically, in the same way the smallest space debris still exerts some nugatory gravitational pull on more important bodies, a nudging which over billions of years may drag a meteor crèching the Adamic nucleobases of RNA/DNA into the path of a water rich asteroid. Of course, fuzzy thought fantasies like these are rare, even in microcosmic biology. A lightning bolt is awe-striking,

---

[73] Assisted suicide, so it seems to me. The Akhuan Civil Arrondissement was diseased, conscripted constitutionalists (25 years of soldiering to qualify for the basest political internship) in demented equilibrium with a Hurricane Democracy which deranged entire countries.

but would anyone call it <u>massy</u>? It might incinerate a fruit fly but do we believe that a fruit fly wobbles due to the gravitational pull of a lightning bolt striking in a different country?

⊕

Ortholog 4: The Invisible Circus

I said the AJPD never causes us to see anything. I should say it was never <u>intended</u> to manifest as vision-auguries, yet twice this breeding factory has inseminated me with eyes whose only function is to <u>see</u> holograms or effigies of estranged friends and exhumed lovers, of famishing student days and nutritious nights in Tinjitan and centipede fire wriggling through the perforated moon gate gardens of Saksiwa. Never has the uncommon "Common Sense" bestowed on us by our Conscript Fathers[74] made me happier. If an ophthalmologist explained to me that a fortuitous family hairpin loop and faulty RNA messaging led to the accidental transmutation of my eye jelly, I would brain myself with a concrete slab to dislodge the memory of such a dispiriting diagnosis. Better head trauma than to desecrate a holy mystery.

⊕

Ortholog 5: The Coagulation Problem

"The Judas Tree grows flowers, spry and spritely purplish."
—The Dissonance Manual

⊕

We speak of Unitarianism when we say <u>Coagulation,</u> a word in Sanhadja which implies the authentic <u>makhzen,</u> a synecdoche

---

[74] Antithetical to the taxidermic mores and putrefacting ethics of the no-minder era, what our Conscript Fathers called, "The coroner's code of conduct. The common sense of a corpse."

for celibate cells which threaten to sterilize the entire body
or the insinuation of a subversive desire for that homogenous
immortality reserved for limestone massifs, fossils and petrified
forests.

    In Sanhadja, Coagulation is high treason. The treasonous
are gelatinized <u>eventually</u> (Sanhadjans are not keen on passing
sentence on Sanhadjans and the criminal is given every chance to
flee[75]). Our most distinguished immigrant and mawla-adoptee
Bint Haruko Tomayashi tells me that this sounds more rewarding
than punishing. With the help of the polity, the criminal has
aspired to and achieved their assimilationist dream. But isn't Hell
our own beguiling body afflicted with apt deformities?

Brood of the Maggot Midwife

Arete is the pursuit of excellence. My hermetic AJPD disposes
me to revere the following paragons of arete, to aspire to the brain
cells of Leonardo Da Vinci, the volcanic heart of a Benvenuto
Cellini, the passionate lucidity of Paul Valéry, the pleb-baiting
patriotism of a John Adams, the muscles of Hercules. To be...the
holographic soul of Edgar Allan Poe shining through the stained-
glass pores of Baudelaire, to be a tracheal megaphone for the
indignant trash talk of a Paracelsus who belonged, like all doctors,
to a suicidal species but was frugal in how he killed himself
(dribbling overtime hours like a strategic martyr).

Paralog 3: Tissue Teleology

The borderless bodies of our northeastern neighbors have become
an obsession with the rising brood of Sanhadjan ethnologists.
More so as the paradoxical Hamajee annexation instinct has only

---

[75] Refer to the 'The Daughters of Didymus,' a <u>brief</u> commonplace book of
disinherited genes.

grown stronger despite their discovery of the outside world and the corollary—the puniness of their former tribal conquests. Of any moral/anatomic symbolism and symbiosis they give zero thought. Their plainspoken enjoyment of plunder pogroms and revengeful ratonnades is not disturbed by the finger wagging of we "megalopolitans of crevice and crèche."[76]

Hamajee muscles and blood vessels are exposed at birth and stay so well into the sorrows of middle age. When their skin begins to erupt...the day of judgment draws near. Debility and dementia are forgivable, but the geriatric skin afflicted by eczema or warts is more inquisition than eulogy, a mosaic of infamy[77] so that the Hamajee are wagging self-evident when they say "the old man unearths what the youth has buried."[78] The skin petrifies swiftly on the corpse which thus functions as its own cairn or coffin.

It is common for travelers, and even for less experienced ethnologists, to mistake for skin that "surgeon's gauze" which sutures their traumatic wounds. Over many days of convalescence the Hamajee sheds, showing no superstitious reverence or sentimentality towards their transient, therapeutic husk. When asked, they pretend to know nothing about the booming "follicle" market or its pestilential husk hunters. Nevertheless, every year a few dozen of these hunters annihilate themselves in fortuitous accidents, which only serves to decimate supply and drive up profits.

---

[76] What must they have thought of Akhua before The Fall, whose budget city-rooms and bathhouses could engulf all 88 (and counting) chaityas of Sanhadja!

[77] What moral monsters might succumb to harlequin disease or leprosy? The Hamajee would not be the only rovers to leave their diseased to die of exposure, though in this case, the caretaking burden on the tribe would only be an incidental motive.

[78] As harsh as that related truism "he who does no work cannot eat." A zero energy organism is not even dead meat, he is "sinks and thinks dissipating like the genius Ada Lovelace into freespace heat and stupid joules."

The Nuptial Gift

There is an idea in Kabbalah that Abraham was sterile until the letter 'He' was added to his name, *le don nuptial*, the gift of fertility, language as auxiliary insemination machine.

Lives of the Sanhadjan Artists

Bint Shamshira

She could look at dunes and see an ocean of glass. She claims each grain is stuffed with microbial stars and ripening planets.[79] Desiccation is the decryption key to Bint Rabïa's art. The paintings in her "Connubial Canon" depict 12 homologous piles of human powder indifferent to the artist's hate or lust. The aesthetic mole who moles bitterly enough, will excavate the subterranean nuptial veins which join pile to pile. Their undulations add up to a seismic shrug, the renunciation of rehydration and putrefaction both.

Jurgurtha Minamoto

A battery fiend who fantasizes about dissolving solid chonks of misbehaving electricity in a drum of acid.

The Epicurean Euthanasiast

The artist-author of *The Nominomicon*. A depressed chef who combines cookery with a genius for assisted suicide.[80]

---

[79] "And soon the fragments dim of lovely forms, come trembling back, unite and now once more—the pool becomes a mirror."

[80] Suicide methods include, *quod aliquando non esse necesseesset*, incessant natural causes.

Last year he unveiled his terminal restaurant project. At the investor presentation his marketing team highlighted the following:

1) A double your money back guarantee of a 40-year tasting menu, with no opt-out clause (save for "acts of God") and a termination bonus on top of the refund should the chef miss more than three consecutive sessions with his therapist.

2) The chef's intimate foreknowledge of the relevant flavor profile.

3) The aura of exclusivity arising organically from the chef's extended recovery time from surgery.

4) Dessert, served by his sous chef, on the Day of Judgment—a synaptic slaw with brined neurons, crème fraîche kidney chonks, and jellied tongue giblets stewed in the chef's stomach acid.

⊕

...then there is Bar Shibli's Museum of Schismatic Heads. Passing by the bread-and-butter schismatics, we arrive at the cortical exhibit dedicated to the Collaborationist Saints, the impresarios whose showmanship-taqiyya was so perfect that through sheer verisimilitude they deluded themselves, to the point of selling out fellow schismatics to allay the suspicions of the orthodox regime. A martyrdom worth of the Gnostic Gospel of Judas as even Bar Shibli, who has dedicated his microbial waseya inheritance and health to his museum, has his doubts whether some of these traitorous martyrs ever snapped out of their tactical brainwashing long enough to execute their original subversions.

In the neighboring gallery we find the Canny Lunatics (the alliterative gallery label proposed by the marketing impresario Bar Labbaan, "The Paragons of Pandemonium," was rejected by the museum board 19 – 0). The exhibits are grouped in vertebral nubs ascending like a spinal cord, with pores in place of doors and a roof which resembles the spider membrane of the brain, while the heads are mounted on pedestals which resemble the bull-neck bodies of martyrs (necks heroically vascular), emaciated martyrs with thirsty ribs impaling their owners or cheeks gnawing on residual cheekbone marrow or sawed-off limbs or entrails yanked out by infidel crocodiles. The heads rarely match with the pedestals. Bar Shibli hesitates to disappoint those guests looking to play "exquisite corpse" and solve the mystery of why neck #6 is supporting head #77, but in private Bar Shibli's ra'wi-curator[81] has admitted to a muckraking arts and lifestyle journalist that Bar Shibli's prime organizational principle is to wait for "divine sparks," each color coded to "feel" like the dominant conundrum or temptation tormenting each saint. Where two sparks land, there Bar Shibli misassembles their respective pedestal.

A representative selection of heads:

Bint Humayuun

She repeated the prayer of John Quincy Adams, that god would defend her against her own mind, a demon whose existence no skeptic could deny. Her ra'wi Bint Husri reverbs that she was "aghast at the confusion of responses which her prayer disturbed." Proof that some Sanhadjans, at the closing of the no-minder era, cursed the wild-seed AJPD inflicted on us by our Conscript Fathers.

Bint Zaidiyya

"Whose mother was the guillotine." Forty years after her execution, her neck was said to splurt milk for the refreshment of the orthodox and wine for infidels.

---

[81] The consecrated civic term ra'wi—echoer-adept*—is used profanely here as a job title in keeping with Bar Shibli's fundraising strategy of offending revanchist *ultras* and thus obligating the *évolué* to hurt their factional rivals by funding Bar Shibli's provocations.

* Can also mean "embellisher-adept," if enterprising.

That Slushy of Saints—The Order of Nesimi

The only "heads" not mounted on a pedestal because liquefied.
A mystic order so fervent for self-annihilation that, by the secret
discipline of their tariqa-order, they slurried their superfluous
bones and lard into a slosh of perfect love.

The Dribbler Bar Saiyidi Ajall

A fragrant mystic who sold his drool as perfume. He was
assassinated by the rival perfumers he bankrupted.

Bar Balkhi

Who plaited his beard to give the orthodox Mob "something to
hang him with."

Bar Hudayj

Circumcised up to the neck, but his facial pores radiated the
supernal searchlight of the beloved murshid, the mystic's guide
into Paradise.

Bint Sintara the Snail

A ramshackle marabout who sutured curling toenails to build
herself a portable snail-house doubling as a mosque.

Lot's Saline Wife

Of doubtful authenticity. The fact that she cradles a salt lick
baby in her arms adds to our suspicion. Voltaire opines that St.
Irenaeus (and Tertullian) "go too far" when they claim that "Lot's
wife still stands in Sodom-land, a menstruating pillar of salt." If
we don't buy that, we can hardly buy that after her transmutation,
a childless and opportunistic Lot coupled with his wife.

The Da'i Al-Mutlaq or Boundless Missionary

A borderless Hamajee ascetic able to one-up rival emaciators by
exhibiting tendons and ligaments scraped of all but sinless lard.

The Emended Eremite Bar Khidr

The saint whose alluring skull the Emperor's constrictor-torturers "emended" to boost the self-esteem of his pet phrenologist who had been mocked by a popular comedian for "prognostic fallacies" leading to suspended treason trials.

The Curator

Bar Shibli has reserved a headless pedestal. He awaits the disciple, "beloved as the guillotine," who reveres the master enough to betray him.

⊕

A Weird Epidemiology

Her protégé and lover publicly called Bint Eshon an aesthetic pandemic infecting/blessing artistic layabouts indiscriminately, but after their breakup she recanted (their repugnant son was denied a plush wasiya legacy in favor of Bint Eshon's niece), confessing that Bint Eshon was "more like pet dander, afflicting only those suffering from hoity-toity allergies."

⊕

Paralog 4: The Toyminder Protocol

An attack piece in *L'Energie*, a hybrid of insurrectional syntax and insinuating technique, the words, in blue organism-ink, age and die and putrefy maliciously. The smell is defamatory.

"A toyminder is a tinkerer. Organisms and machines interest him equally. He can take nothing seriously—not science, upheavals, atrocity—unless he makes a game of it. All that's necessary is that he competes with somebody. That much achieved, he states sincerely. 'The finest effort of human beings is rule balancing and to hire impartial referees.'"

Paralog 5: The Analects of Bar Sanjil

Quoted in *L'Bradeur*, the sellout's magazine:

"All men are made of time, shedding skin-cell hours, all may-or-maybes, all reliable and unreliable daydreams. That's what it means—senility. To be...a residue of body and body language without ambience or chronology."

⊕

Allele 1: Our Stupid Destiny[82]

> They were like the prince who trembled at the sight of a comet, and said gravely to those who did not fear it, "You may behold it without concern, you are not princes."
> —Voltaire, *Philosophical Dictionary*

⊕

> There exist three books: *The Vivisections of God, The Book of Nature*, which Paracelsus worshipped, and that adored, abhorred by us, *The Book of Blood*, the Ajami Private Diction.
> —Bar Junayd, *The Worship Manual*

⊕

The general illiteracy of the coming era had two doubtful virtues. A man could aspire to all knowledge. To increase human stupidity was impossible.

A library of a hundred volumes, growing century to century by two redundant volumes, threatens no one. And though the

---

[82] Reproduced, with permission, from "The Patchwork Compendium, Episcript 333."

risk of novelty was greater than zero, in the short run there were no new thoughts, only ideas like stars, eternally revolving back to start.

In our own era, the Ajami <u>Public</u> Diction[83] and the Cacophony—with their hideous mutation and emanation of data—have demolished this sterile epistemology, while paradoxically undermining our faith in human genius.

Entire libraries congeal from a drop of Sanhadjan blood. A cosmos erupts from a deeper cut. A single mouth of the Cacophony can process three bodies per dyadic year. The "Index" of Bar Shuqayr enumerates 4,000,022 mouths. His grandson, my childhood tutor, is still counting.

Overawed by this godlike gibbering—the mouths strike deals to slander unallied mouths—some worship the cacophony as god. The heresiarch Hudayj remarks that god "appears drunk on his own blood." No less repulsive, or comical, is the image of a living factory for the reproduction of prophetic lips and tongues, other parts being expendable,[84] the Ajami <u>Private</u> Diction—its raw material, a molecular scripture and predestiny.[85]

Our citizens enslave themselves. Every question must be submitted to the Cacophony, including whether to consult

---

[83] Bar Eshon argues that the AJPD was meant to preserve freedom, not data. A personal and fallible guide which would deny those afflicted the safety, or tyranny, of "common knowledge" and could never excuse them from the agony of thought.

[84] A pious parody: Cenote Lancôme has since "trimmed" their staff of contract perfumers and now employs upwards of 888 severed sensile noses.

[85] It was my grandfather who first asked the Cacophony how we might destroy it or at least exterminate the accursed race of Sanhadjans whose veins supply its raw data. For once all mouths did concur, but only to confirm that the Cacophony is invulnerable and has already devoured enough monomers to answer a million generation's worth of petitions. We have since resigned ourselves to the following conjecture: As only Cacophony can make sense of the inexhaustible nonsense of the Ajami <u>Private</u> Diction, it follows that the AJPD can omit nothing but how to destroy Cacophony.

Cacophony or whether other mouths have lied. Each response must be transcribed for fear that a single omission may lead to disaster. Many polymerists have starved, lest they falter in this infernal struggle. Others the mob have burned alive for a single typo. We have even been told that scribes have murdered fellow scribes rather than risk exposure of their future errors. At least the Cacophony suggests such betrayals are possible.

The proportion of known to knowable approaches null. As the organic prison of Kerkur swells, according to subversive gossip, with the admission of every political criminal, so our libraries expand beyond an immortal librarian's ability to catalog.[86]

The best grow paralyzed. Bored, the worst invent new crimes or commit deeds of pointless heroism. Entire populations herd and trample each other, abandoning, repossessing their homes in a single hour. Farmers plant a square kos but only harvest a haath. Beggars steal the withering crops but let themselves starve. Industrialists build factories for the production of jobs and competitors. Our restauranteurs manufacture surplus stomachs for their ulcerating patrons. Laws are enacted in imaginary languages. Comedians enforce the law. Men establish revolutionary tribunals to restore the ancient regime. No sin is worth committing or avoiding. All virtues are celebrated, reviled. Every sage is presaged, every presage confirmed. Immediately, or eventually, every presage is refuted.

---

[86] The "Immateria" speaks of 30,000 demons carving blasphemies across a pinhead. A single mouth of the Cacophony has elucidated 50 million antithetical chemical laws—a second mouth doubts the first mouth exists, a third claims that the search for universal principles is evil—contrary to what our physical reality allows, by which microbial astronomers chart twinkling pinhead demons as stars or giants diffuse their cells in gaseous city-states ruled by protonic senators. In some may-or-may-not worlds, all men breathe through a single lung or build epidermal houses whose morbid obesity have incited more than one dietary fad. In others, men colonize other men.

Of less cosmic concern, the Cacophony has revealed to me my 888 faithless brides. At other times, I am the bride, or an adulterer, or a venerated celibate, or faithfulness is a crime.

Idiocy appears inescapable, though I dare to hope that from the foreceding era it may yet come down to us that the essential desire of The Wise will be for annihilation. Their beautiful action—to counterfeit each other so precisely that man and his thoughts merge in the bewildered mouths of god. Who, unable to distinguish itself from its own creation or even to describe itself, god, it's oracles, our stupid destiny—disappear.

Gonadal Glyphs

ا — Adenine, the Adamic single-cell.

ق — Cytosine. The Borderless Body.

غ — Guanine. Ratiocinated harmonies or harmonic absurdities.

ط — Thymine. Knowledge, bidden and forbidden, the enigma of epistemology.

و — Uracil. The Ummat. The Ahl Al-Hadith.

ACKNOWLEDGEMENTS

"Funeral Stories" was first published in *The Ex-Puritan*.

"An Unpublished Obituary" was first published in *Midway Journal*.

"Dipygus" was first published in *Western Humanities Review*.

"Selves of Themselves" was first published in *Isthmus*.

"The Mouth of the Word" was first published in *STORGY*.

"The Girls Guide to Ghost Fucking" was first published in *Carousel*.

"The Patchwork Compendium" was first published in *Harpur Palate*.

"The Stars in Middle Age" was first published in *The Collidescope*.